Heart to Heart ♥ Forever

*To Janice &
Lewis,
You never know!
Zoom - where have
the years gone.
Enjoy!
Love,
Kay
8-15-08*

By Kay Blanks

Heart to Heart ♥ Forever

©2008 Kay Blanks

All Rights Reserved

This book is a work of fiction. Names, characters, places and incidents are products of the author's imagination or are used fictitiously. Any resemblance to actual events or persons, living or dead, is entirely coincidental.

No part of this publication may be reproduced or transmitted in any other form or for any means, electronic or mechanical, including photocopy, recording or any information storage system, without written permission from the author.

For More Information Visit
www.kayblanks.com

ISBN: 0-929915-83-6
ISBN 13: 978-0-929915-83-8

Library of Congress Control Number: 2008931873

Printed in the United States of America

Dedication

Andrea Kay

    My forty-two year-old daughter Andrea has been fighting breast cancer for nearly eight years. This book is dedicated to her—not because of the disease but because of her, the kind of woman she is. She has inspired me her entire life with her extreme girly-girl ways. She is the epitome of the kind of gal this book is about. Andrea has kept me young in mind and spirit with all her energy and excitement for life.

    Baby girl, this one's for you. I love you.

Mama

A percentage of the sale of each book will be donated by the author to Susan G. Komen for the Cure, 5005 LBJ Freeway, Suite 250, Dallas, TX 785244, Tel: (888) 888-3317 FAX: (972) 855-1605

Acknowledgments

This book is proof that anyone can write a book. My dear mother often said, "Kay has all the talent." Mama was an avid reader and would be so proud of her "little girl."

My husband and soul mate of forty years sat beside me every night playing poker as I created each character, then read him bits and pieces. Our children are anxious to see the finished product and my awesome older grandchildren have actually been involved with developing character and scenes.

And how can I ever thank my wonderful g'friends that inspired me throughout Heart to Heart~ Forever? There would never have been a book had it not been for City Elaine, Country Elaine, Fay-Z, Cousin Billie, and Mame—thank you, ladies!

To my friends who took time to proof this book along the way and cheered me to the finish line: I owe you. And a special thanks to my newest friend, Sandy, my editor, who probably wanted to pull her hair out at times. But I know we will be friends forever.

Thanks to you for reading my first attempt, I hope you enjoy it. I want to become your worst habit and look forward to hearing from you at my personal website www.kayblanks.com or my personal blog at www.kayblanks/blog.

Blessings to all,
Kay

Chapter 1

Frigid winds howled down out of the Northwest, spun off the flanks of the Colorado Rockies, whirled free and angry across the Great Plains, and made their way south into Texas. The winds escorted the blue norther with nasty needlepoint sleet as it bullied its way into Silver Springs. The eight-degree temperature threatened to plummet even farther; it was the worst winter storm this year.

Jettie McNamara peeked out to check the conditions; she was the last to leave their store, The Furniture Showcase. Her husband Toby had left earlier to make bank deposits and save her the hassle with the weather. There would be lines in every lane all the way out to Main Street. Texans were spoiled with eighty degrees in mid-December and didn't like to deal with the icy weather this storm dictated. After Toby, the employees had disappeared one car after the other like jets airborne at Dallas Fort Worth Airport, a trail of exhaust fumes the only reminder they'd even been there. Friday, end of their workweek—but most important to the staff—payday!

Her mind set to face the elements, Jettie yanked on the wool cap, clutched the front of her coat, ducked her head, and made a run for it. Her cheeks stung from the prickly ping of sleet. She opened the door to the white Caddy and jumped inside. The engine turned over smoothly, and while it warmed, she sat there a few minutes. Her cap no longer needed, she slipped it off and, with icy fingers, tousled her signature blond hair.

Satisfied with the coif, she adjusted the radio and backed out. She eased onto the frozen highway and hunkered down with both hands on the wheel. Captivated by the rare sight of the snowy scene reminiscent of a Norman Rockwell painting, Jettie admired Mother Nature's landscape art. She marveled at the city that had been hijacked by the season. She imagined fireplaces crackling and embers aglow as they danced on the walls of the snow-covered cottages.

She cut through the area known as Silk Stocking Row. The locals had named it thus decades ago due to the number of wealthy residents. Swirls of smoke belched from the chimneys, then trailed into the darkened sky, leaving behind the smell of burning wood as the final curtain of eve began its descent.

Jettie remained alert as she maneuvered the Caddy home; it was dependable and comfortable like an old friend. Her house resembled a giant snowball. She opted to park close to the curb to avoid the icy patch that promised to sink her new red boots. Jettie had just a few more steps to the porch covered thick with snow. Aha! Last step; she was almost home free!

The arctic blast with its icy fingers pinched at her face; her neck scarf danced in the air. The storm had grown more treacherous by the hour. Her eyes watered, making it impossible to see where to insert the key. Annoyed, she dabbed at them with gloved fingers. Joy, her best friend, had called earlier. Jettie had been up to her eyeballs in payroll and workers waiting for early dismissal, hoping to beat the worst of the storm home. She had been unable to focus on the conversation while Joy vented.

Yes! The key slid into position. The massive door swung open. "Hallelujah!" Jettie shut the door and leaned back to catch her breath, thrilled to be safely home. The scent of cinnamon filled the air. This home was Paradise to them so thirty-five years ago they named it Shangri-La—and now it welcomed her back. With the concerns of the world on the other side of the door, she could focus on Joy's situation. In automatic mode, she placed her keys on the wall rack and walked straight ahead, flipping lights on as she passed.

Jettie tossed her favorite over-sized T-shirt and fluffy house slippers in the dryer. She wiggled out of her work clothes and after a few minutes, reached into the dryer for the toasty night shirt and slipped it over her head. Next she poured a cup of hot Chai tea and inhaled the delicious aroma of spice. In the den, she settled her 5'4" frame into the comfy queen's chair and tucked her cold tootsies under the fur cover; in heaven, at last.

Jettie eased her tense neck back onto the cushion and closed her eyes. This could not be happening; it was a soap opera. She rubbed her neck; the muscles were as tight as a fiddle string. Her heart ached knowing the humiliation Joy would suffer. Sharp tongues in a small town could be vicious. She wished Frank were there so she could slap him into tomorrow.

She wanted to do something to ease her friend's pain. After all, they had been friends their entire lives, through thick and thin. They were two peas in a pod. As girls they were total opposites; Joy's long hair had been jet black and her curvy body matured before Jettie's. Jettie had been blond even without the help of L'Oreal. Joy was quieter, more reserved, while Jettie was an outgoing social butterfly. They say that opposites attract, and that was definitely the case for these two girls.

Joy and Frank had met after Joy's break up with Vince. Jettie always thought that Joy had married on the rebound. Frank was quiet, dark and handsome with perfect white teeth. Their marriage had produced one daughter, Jules, the spitting image of her mother, who had married her high school sweetheart, Chauncey. He was tall, thin, blond and studious. He wore glasses but they did not make him appear a geek. Chauncey got lucky when he had the opportunity to buy out a retiring dentist.

Jules had been recently accepted at Berman, Bailey & Associates—a well respected law firm in the city.

Jettie took the last sip of tea, then remembered she'd promised to call Dixie. They agreed a heart-to-heart was in order. The girly-girl get-togethers had provided counsel over many years, and it was their way to stay in touch and reel each other in.

Jettie speed-dialed Dixie May's beauty shop, the Magic Touch, and a recorder answered. "Meet us at the Enchanted Gardens for a heart-to-heart on Monday," Jettie said. "Joy has news of Frank, and it's going to blow your hat in the creek."

The final member of the heart-to-heart bunch, Krystal, a tall blond who was always on the arm of her equally tall and slender husband Johnny, was out of town. Krystal and Johnny often traveled on road trips with their Harley group. They would be back in a week, and Jettie decided to fill her in on the latest when she returned.

Impatient, Jettie walked past the window and pulled back the drapes. She hoped to catch a glimpse of her man, but he was nowhere in sight. At sixty-four, Toby was still handsome, and the extra forty pounds he'd gained over the years didn't detract from his good looks. Women found him attractive. He was a workaholic, starting every morning on the phone beside his bed. After his shower, he would comb his full head of salt and pepper hair, then slide his watch on with the face turned to the inside of his wrist. She used to wonder in the early years why he wore it that way. After kissing her goodbye, he headed to the door but not before giving her an instruction or two for the day. He'd always been in business for himself, never an eight-to-five kind of guy.

It was now dark outside, and no one except for the diehards who wouldn't give it up still fought the elements. Jettie wanted Toby home now, so they could get "denned in." Her stomach growled—lunch had been peanut butter and crackers. As soon as he walked in they would eat and she would tell him of Joy's dilemma, then retire to the den. As always, Toby channel surfed between Texas Hold-Em, and CSI. She planned to sink into the sofa that felt like a cloud, and drift in and out of slumber.

Car lights flashed across the window; at last, Toby was home. Jettie dashed into the kitchen and punched the microwave button to zap her homemade chicken soup. She grabbed two glasses and filled them with ice from the fridge door, then poured tea. Dinner was on the table by the time Toby parked his truck and walked into the foyer.

"Woman, is my dinner ready?" he shouted. "The man of the house is home!"

Jettie chuckled. She knew the man like a book. She went to greet the love of her life. She turned the corner to see him remove his jacket, then hang it on the coat rack. From the back, she caught him off guard and wrapped him in a bear hug. With her face pressed to his shirt, she could smell the crisp cold air that clung to his clothes. He tried to touch her with his icy hands but she jumped and said, "Watch out! You know better than that." He persisted playfully, and she jumped again. "Don't you dare, or I'll hurt you bad." She pointed her finger. "Now follow me; soup's on."

Amused, he did as she ordered. He first washed his hands, then took his chair at the kitchen table. Toby buttered his hot cornbread as Jettie ladled steamy soup into their bowls.

Jettie leaned back in her chair. "You won't believe what Joy found today," she said.

"What's that?"

Jettie made an exaggerated wink. "Joy accidentally knocked Frank's daytimer off the desk this morning."

Frank picked up on the look. "Yeah?"

"And a picture fell out."

Toby looked puzzled. "A picture?"

"Yes. A picture of a Latino woman and two boys."

Toby stared at Jettie, a confused look on his face.

"Two boys—around six and eight years old—who look identical to Frank. Identical, Toby! Like clones." She waited while the news sunk in.

"You don't mean—"

"Yes, that is exactly what I mean. Frank is a scoundrel. Can you believe the nerve of that guy? He and Joy have only been divorced for two years. Toby, that means he fathered these kids while he was still married to—and living with—Joy. The jerk."

Toby swallowed his last spoonful of soup and pushed the bowl back. "Sounds like we never knew the real Frank, did we?"

"That's a fact." She tried to say more, say how angry and betrayed she felt for her friend, but words couldn't escape. She squeezed her eyes tightly to keep the tears from overflowing. She wiped her tears; her feathers were ruffled.

Toby reached over and patted her on the shoulder. "Sweetheart, don't cry. Believe it or not, everything will work out."

"I know. I just hurt for her. I just hope it won't make her feel that her life has been wasted, and all their years together meant nothing—that not even the birth of Jules…. Oh, Toby, it's hard to explain how a woman feels." She dabbed her eyes with her napkin. "I've only spoken to Joy by phone. I won't see her until Monday. She sounded okay, but I have to call in a little while just to check on her."

Toby sat like a rock and listened, silent and strong; he patiently allowed her to vent and get it all out.

"Later, Joy and I may have to snoop and find out where Frank's secret family resides." Now feeling inspired, she pointed her spoon at him. "Yes! That will be the plan."

Toby took a drink of tea. "Frank is doomed if you two discover his hideout."

"You're right!" She jumped up to gather the bowls for the dishwasher. "I could tell Frank and his senorita a thing or two about bringing those innocent little boys into this disgraceful affair! He should be hung, drawn and quartered!"

Toby stood. He leaned over and hugged her. "Be careful. Walk softly and carry a big stick, but by all means, keep your opinions to yourself, my dear." Pleased with himself and his stick comment, he laughed boisterously. He aimed to make light of the situation and make his wife feel better at the same time. Before he left the room, he hugged and kissed her. "Supper was good." When he got to the doorway, he stopped. "Sweetheart, I am very sorry about Joy's situation. I know how bad this upsets you. And I forgot to ask, has she told Jules?"

"Thanks, sweetie. She didn't say and I didn't ask."

Frank Hillary had a lot of little boy ways that endeared him to the friends' mothers because he liked to eat. He was a big teddy bear, and they were all taken by surprise by the breakup.

Once the dishes were done and the kitchen back in order, Jettie returned to the den and phoned her friend. She punched up her pillow with her fists and crawled onto the sofa again, then tucked the fur under her toes. Toby reared back in his leather La-Z-Boy recliner. Neither would last long. Settled into their nest, Jettie put away her cell. "Joy sounded okay; she was already in bed."

"You know she goes to bed with the chickens," Frank teased.

Jettie reached for the remote control; like magic, the fireplace leaped to life. The lights danced as the fire flickered while Old Man Winter held Silver Springs captive. The night grew colder, but in Shangri-Li, it was cozy. The soul mates were snug in the security and warmth of home, like two bears hibernating deep in a cave for the long winter months.

Jettie sighed, a sigh of satisfaction. She and Toby were some of the lucky ones; their romance had been sprinkled with magic dust. Married for thirty-six years, they'd had to work through the rough spots during the early years, but later their relationship grew stronger each year. The couple kept their noses to the grindstone, and it paid off for them. Their store, The Furniture Showcase, was going strong. They had just rolled out the red carpet to mark their tenth anniversary. The couple hosted a big bash and set up a stage for a live band in the parking lot. All the hoopla kept the community buzzing for months after the celebration.

A fireworks display had been a hit for the second time around. An imported French designer armoire was given away when the drawing ticket was called at the close of the evening. A surprised true-blue customer won. The winner sang praises for the elaborate gift and the McNamaras' generosity everywhere he went for months. Word of mouth had always been the best advertisement, and the McNamara's knew it. They knew how to keep their customers happy.

Jettie's specialty was public relations and special events; nobody was better at working a crowd than she. The wine and cheese flowed, as did the sales receipts. Jettie's flair to stage an event had worked again and loosened the purse strings of the many attendees. She and Toby's partnership was key to their continued success. The business decision for her to leave behind a lucrative twenty-year real estate career had been a wise move. Together the pair had the eye of the tiger—Toby's business savvy and Jettie's edge for marketing and design; they were survivors. "Toby has his fingers in everything from sales to warehouse deliveries," Jettie laughingly said. "He won't let anybody make a decision without him."

His reputation gained him a lot of respect throughout the industry. The man was a born entrepreneur and taught Jettie to be. "He owned a car lot at eighteen-years-old and a body shop at twenty. Now you know how unusual that is; the man is a piece of work," she told her customers. They were the epitome of the dynamic duo and complemented each other.

Toby's snores interrupted Jettie's reverie. She smiled. Yes, she was the lucky one.

Chapter 2

Dixie May always ran late, and today was no exception. She leaned over to the rearview mirror, checked her teeth for lipstick, then glanced at her watch. Eight-fifteen—not bad with the amount of sleep she'd had after her date. Just remembering the date and Chet gave her a thrill in the pit of her stomach.

Mr. James Brown wailed over the radio, "I Feel Good," an oldie but goodie that never got too old. Dixie enjoyed a wide range of music; she sang along, "I feel good and I knew that I would…"

Dixie was a sassy woman with long red hair. She was one of those folks who were timeless and seemed to never age. Her energy level and attitude had been the recipe for remaining youthful when the other part of her life failed her. She had always been able to bounce back and seemed to never be out of step with the world of style. On many occasions she scolded her best friends, "Never, ever call yourself old; it is negative. It's not in my vocabulary." She wheeled her yellow Firebird up to the front door of her beauty shop and stopped with a squeal of the tires. The only person out and about was the scrooge landlord, after the almighty dollar. She grimaced. "Brother, he should get a life."

With the door unlocked, she glanced over her shoulder. Peter Winn, her landlord who owned another building across the street, glanced her way. She threw up her hand in a wave and proceeded into the shop.

The red light blinked on the phone, signaling a message. It got her attention. She punched the "on" button and kept walking. It was Jettie's voice. "We need to get together on Monday at the Enchanted Gardens. Joy has news of Frank that will blow your hat in the creek."

What in the world? Joy and Frank had been divorced for two years. Dixie couldn't imagine what the news could be. Today was

Saturday; it would be a couple of days before she met the girls. Her curiosity was piqued; she had to call Jettie later. Mrs. White would blow in that door any minute. Dixie hadn't even gotten the thought from her mind, when the door bell jingled.

Mrs. White chirped, "Good morning, Dixie May." Dixie greeted her, then motioned her to the shampoo bowl.

Trudy hadn't made it in yet, but Dixie May was fast and would have two heads under the dryer before Trudy arrived and poured her first cup of coffee. Trudy assisted with shampoos when Dixie May was snowed under. She was booked every thirty minutes until five. To make it all run smoothly and keep her feeling well, she would grab a bite to eat between comb-outs.

Mrs. White was the first on Dixie's long list of customers for the day. She was as faithful to her weekly hair appointment as she had been to her position as principal at the elementary school for the past fifteen years.

Dixie May owned and operated the Magic Touch Beauty Salon with the help of her two stylist's. After she'd divorced Eddie Carlton twelve years ago, she bought the beauty salon. Eddie had been the worst. What a loser; the man wouldn't keep a job. She still wondered what had possessed her to marry him. He would be the end of the line for marriages. Dixie promised, "The only vow I'll be taking is the vow to never depend on another man for anything."

It was Dixie's habit to open the salon, make coffee and have a load of towels in the dryer before anyone else arrived. The customers, spoiled by her magic hands, watched her create many a silk purse out of a sow's ear. She had made that remark too many times to count over the years. And everybody thought it was cute! And even when people called her a beauty operator, she would remark, "Now, I don't get to work on many beauties." If anyone else talked that way, it would have been the kiss of death.

It felt great to be boss, and the title gave her a lot of respect. Dixie couldn't think of anything she enjoyed more than greeting the familiar faces each week. Never bored—quite the contrary. Over the years she'd gotten to know every family she serviced. At Christmas she received so many gifts from her customers she had to build additional storage in her home for the abundance. She had most of the ritzy trade when it came to the wives of the doctors, lawyers and other professionals. They were generous with her and didn't spare the checkbook when it came to their looks.

In the small cattle town, her shop also reigned as the hot spot for hair design with the high school crowd. The young teen hopefuls were in competition for Miss Silver Springs. If lucky, the next step would be Miss Texas. These teensters wouldn't dare be seen in a salon that didn't offer the latest trends, highlights, lowlights and foil techniques. And they wouldn't dream of being caught dead in an "old lady's beauty shop." The Magic Touch was the trendiest shop in town. The customers stood in line to book Star; she was the freshest talent for the younger folks and the newest top stylist in the city.

Trudy's expertise was nail art, and she assisted the other two with various duties. "I don't try to make a name for myself. I work strictly for the money, not popularity," she said.

Dixie had always carried the torch—until Star came to town. All the stylists attended the Dallas hair shows. Dixie was a creature of habit, and she had a cleaning service that came on Mondays when they were closed. She required very little of the operators, only to keep the towels cleaned and folded and the hair swept up.

The increase in prices last summer hadn't slowed them down. "Oh well," Dixie said, "I have no complaints." Between running the shop and catering to Chet, she didn't have time to powder her nose.

Dixie responded to the ding of Mary Perkins' dryer. She lifted the top and said, "Let's go, Mary. I know you have some swamp land to sell." She winked at the real estate guru. Again, only Dixie May could make statements like that and get away with it. Rolling off someone else's tongue, the same words would sound like a downright insult.

Mary Perkins was past middle-age and still the real estate queen of Chapel Valley. On occasion, new agents got their names in the papers, but it was Mary's name that came to mind when you thought about buying or selling. Her hairstyle never varied. It was always the same—boring. It was okay with Dixie; she could have her combed out in five minutes. Dixie hummed and never missed a roller as she plucked them from Mary's hair.

In a flash, Mary was settled in her big silver Lincoln, cell phone in hand, en route to a closing. Dixie told the customer still in the salon, "You have to admire that woman; she has tunnel vision, and when she has someone bird-dogged, she doesn't take her eye off them until they sign on the dotted line."

Dixie May was still the fastest comb in the East, but her personality was similar to Dolly Parton's and just as funny.

What a day! Dixie plopped down in her chair and tossed her comb into the style tray after her last customer walked out the door. She wanted to chill out a few minutes before the operators started to work on her. It felt good to sit. She grabbed a brush and threw her head between her knees and brushed her hair vigorously; then roughed it up with both hands. That felt good and seemed to prime her for the rejuvenating shampoo.

"Hey, Trudy, run the pedicure bath, and set up my manicure, please, ma'am."

Trudy was a forty-five-ish, good natured woman. She'd been widowed for five years but never spoke about her husband. Her naturally curly brown hair required very little attention. She could shampoo and blow it dry, and it looked great. The high arch of her brows accented Trudy's wide set hazel eyes and you never saw her without lipstick. She did her work and went home every night to her man, Mr. Kitty. She said, "He is loyal and greets me at my door every evening, then demands all my undivided attention."

Dixie May looked forward to a manicure, pedicure, facial, hair color and style at the end of her long day. The two operators promised to pamper and mold her into her finest. She had another hot date with the heartthrob, and she didn't want to disappointment him.

Before going to the back with the operators, she decided to start a fresh load of towels; then she could put them in the dryer while her color was processing.

Star had blocked enough time from her appointment book to color Dixie's hair. They concocted a beautiful color combination that would light up the night in a flaming red, with just the right hues to add depth. Star's name fit her to a T; she was a star in the business. Dixie knew her good fortune when she managed to snag her right out of beauty school. The senior students were allowed to book appointments in the school exactly as a licensed operator could, so she graduated with a client base that took most operators years to build. On occasion, Dixie May would visit the local beauty school and have her hair done or some service performed. She was there for one reason, and that was to see the new talent, if there was any.

Trudy promised her a full body massage, a treat they performed for each other when the occasion arose. After all this attention, Dixie would be transformed into a little lump of sugar that Chet Tyler's sweet tooth couldn't resist. Plans with Chet included a romantic dinner and dancing. Conway Twitty sang, "You Want a Man with a Slow Hands." And Dixie agreed whole-heartedly. But this man would have to be handled just right, lassoed and taken down real slow and easy. She had to hold him back, make him want her, need her, tease him and please him, and finally, make him want to keep her.

While Dixie surrendered to the attention of Trudy and Star, her mind replayed the old days. It had been her talent to attract difficult situations. She married Joe Tom Powell, the varsity cheerleader, straight after graduation in May. He was an outstanding athlete, a great gymnast, and an amazing acrobatic leader on the ball field. She was bowled over by his talent. Together, their personalities made them one of the cutest couples in the senior class. They drove with friends to Oklahoma, a trend of the times, and wed in front of a justice of the peace. Joe Tom went to work in his father's insurance office; it would one day be his. They set up house, then played house for a year. She and Joe Tom had dated most of her senior year, but that did not qualify them to commit to a lifetime of marriage. It ended as fast as it began. Decades later, a psychologist would point out to Dixie that she had married in search of acceptance, due to the dysfunctional lifestyle with her mother.

Next, Dixie met Rubin when she waited tables in a busy restaurant by the highway. The tips were generous. Rubin was aggressive and personable, a sharp dresser and a smooth talker. This perfect formula often won him salesman of the month. Rubin's silver tongue was smooth enough to sweep Dixie May off her feet. He proposed, and she accepted. They took their vows at a small church with a handful of family, peppered with a few of their friends. They located an apartment and created a home in the tiny space. They were okay for five years. Then one night, with no emotion, Rubin pulled the rug out from under her. Point blank, after supper, he announced, "I've found someone else I intend to marry, and I want a divorce." He stood there and picked his teeth.

Dixie stood at the sink and washed dishes. She felt her heart stop. She couldn't look at him. He had met someone all right: prissy little Kari Courtney, a spoiled rotten rich girl. She was the daughter of old man Courtney, a cattle baron in the area, and he was loaded. Anything Kari wanted, Kari got. Daddy bought her a car, and that's when Rubin came into her focus. His tall straight posture and gift of gab bedazzled Kari; he was different from the high school and college boys. Not only did Kari get the convertible, she got the salesman. She strutted around in those short shorts and baby-talked Rubin into submission. He was tired of being on the clock, and he wanted to ride the fast train—the Courtney Express, to be exact. He wanted to be a big shot and didn't care who he boarded on the train. Dixie, just as matter of fact, told him he could have his divorce, but she wanted money for a cosmetology course. Rubin didn't hesitate; he took out his checkbook and filled in the full amount.

Dixie May cried for the first month, but when she stopped, it was over. She never let him see her down. She vowed no man would ever do that to her again.

The divorce was final in sixty days.

Dixie signed up the next day for Greenville Beauty School. She attended five days a week and worked the restaurant on weekends. She had no desire to date. She had been burned twice and enough was enough.

In nine months, she completed the course and graduated. Her hairdressing license was the single most important thing she had ever wanted and achieved by herself. Jettie and Joy treated her to lunch to celebrate the big news. Jettie sneaked her license out, and the girls had it matted and brass-framed, then surprised her with it at lunch. Dixie cried, but this time it was happy tears.

The salon she preferred hired her on the spot. She moved in her supplies and set up her station. With pride she hung her new license, and then stood back to look at it. She felt a great sense of pride and achievement with her name on that wall. Being the new girl, she would have to prove her talent, and that meant taking whatever walked in the door. "Oh well, I've always enjoyed a challenge."

She started on the busiest day of the week, Saturday, and she was the center of attention all day. A woman walked in with three small boys in need of haircuts. The other operators got their kicks as they watched the greenhorn do the least desirable job in a shop: children who wouldn't keep still! To their surprise, Dixie sailed through the cuts like a seasoned pro. The mother was so pleased she gave Dixie May a generous tip. At the end of the day, Dixie May had eight confirmed appointments for the next week and a healthy chunk of change in her pocket.

Years later, a client told her of Rubin's divorce. After a ten year marriage, Kari replaced him with her tennis instructor; she seemed to like his strokes better.

Dixie hooted and said, "It sounds to me like old Rubin was thrown off the 'Courtney Express'!"

"Yes, and now he's back in used cars at the Acme Cars to Go, where he started as a youngster for his uncle," informed her client. That laugh was good for her soul; justice had been served.

She worked in local beauty shops for twenty-five years, and along the way, she met and married Eddie Carlton, her third and final husband. They divorced after only nine months. Dixie couldn't tolerate his laziness and inability to hold onto a job.

Then Dixie got lucky with the opportunity of a lifetime—to buy her own salon. It happened, it was meant to be, and it had been her pride and joy ever since.

Chapter 3

Joy placed her wine order. She was the first to arrive and thought wine was appropriate for the occasion. Her recent discovery of her ex-husband's hidden family remained on her mind. She thought it might do her good to scream at the top of her lungs, but, oh well, instead she told the waitress to bring her a glass. She had to relieve the stress in her neck, which felt like a twisted rope. The others could order when they arrived.

Jettie joined her, and together they watched Dixie May pull into the lot. Joy was pleased; it warmed her heart to know that Dixie would make the sacrifice to drive forty miles to Silver Springs on her day off. "Girls," she said as she approached the table, "I should've kept my tired butt in bed and ate bonbons, but I had to come see what was going on."

Jettie and Joy stood up to greet Dixie May with hugs and cheek kisses. They all spoke at the same time. Jettie threw her hands in the air, and said, "Girls, please, let's sit down." Jettie had been anxious and restless ever since she realized what had happened and that it included innocent children.

Joy pulled out her chair. "Yes, let's sit down. Bear in mind that once I tell this story, I don't want to talk about it again. I'm sick of it. It's all I've thought about for the last forty-eight hours. And we all have better things to think about, which you'll agree once you've heard this."

Dixie removed her purse and camera from her shoulder and placed them on the back of her chair. "Remind me to take pictures before we leave. But, let's place our order. Rarely do I get to sit down and eat." She pointed to the table beside them. "That Trio Combo looks good; shall we make it easy and get one of those?" They agreed.

Dixie flagged down the waitress. "Marie, we'll have three Trio Combos, please. And when we're finished, one order of strawberry shortcake with three forks. It's my treat, ladies; I've had a good week."

Marie scribbled their order on a pad, then tucked her pencil behind her ear. "I'll take care of everything, ladies. Glad to see ya'll today!"

The trio said in unison, their usual, "It's great to be seen!"

Marie smiled. "Enjoy your day, ladies."

Joy cleared her throat. All eyes were on her. "Okay, ya'll know what's been up for the last two years. The shrink, the couch, the divorce, getting to know myself and accepting the person I am, and then the volunteer work. Right? Well, about the time I think this epic is about to wind down, here we go again!"

Jettie reached across the table and squeezed Joy's hand.

Joy took a deep breath. "I still don't believe this is my life." It was difficult for her to say the words, but she forged ahead. "The same man I shared my bed with for twenty-nine of the best years of my life has turned out to be a total stranger. The marriage that resulted in the miraculous birth of our beautiful Jules is a farce." Joy closed her eyes.

Dixie and Jettie looked at each other. They knew Joy needed a moment to get it together, so they waited.

Joy opened her eyes and took another deep breath. "It's hard for me to verbalize what I am about to say, so I will just spit it out. Frank Hillary—" She toyed with her napkin. "The low life dog, the pig . . ." Joy wadded the napkin in her fist. "The man I loved for a lifetime, cheated on me." She let go of the napkin, then smoothed the wrinkles with her hand. "Not only did he cheat on me when I thought all was well, he created another family while married to me! He is a work of art, pure trash! A bigamist, no less!"

Dixie, mouth agape, blinked several times, then opened her mouth. "You are right, Jettie. This blows my hat in the creek, honey!"

Joy, her cheeks flushed, spoke with passion and pain. "He had the balls to have a family with another woman—two children!" She tore the napkin to shreds. "Then, I stumbled upon a photo of the other woman Friday morning when I went by the old house."

Joy stopped with the napkin and folded her hands in her lap. Minutes dragged by. Never had there been silence between these women. Jettie, who was never speechless, was today. All the color had drained from Dixie's well-painted face.

Dixie stood up, and hugged Joy's head to her waist and stroked her hair. "Dear friend, you are going to be just fine." She took a tissue and wiped the mascara from under Joy's eyes.

Joy smiled and said, "I love you, Dixie May."

Dixie smiled. "I know," she said and returned to her chair. "What about Jules; what does she say?" Dixie poured herself a glass of water.

Joy shook her head. "She's quiet, and I don't know what to make of her reaction. But I called Frank and told him to meet me at our lawyer's office yesterday. He asked what was up, and I said, 'There have been some changes, and we need to take care of them.' One of Jules' associates will handle it for us. I don't want to involve her. I told him I wanted the house sold immediately, and he seemed surprised. Then he asked if it had anything to do with his day-timer he'd found on the floor. I glared at him square in the eyes and spit, 'Damn right, Daddy.' Then he crumbled like a sand castle. Tears filled his eyes, but he never once muttered that he was sorry. He spilled his guts, admitted the affair." Joy made quotation marks in the air for emphasis, "For ten years. They met on a job and became friends," she said, exaggerating the word.

Jettie rolled her eyes. "Oh, yeah. The old friend thing."

"He and Pilar plan to marry so they can be family for little Emilio, six, and Estevan, eight."

"Damn," Dixie said and shook her head. "I thought a lot of bizarre things had happened to me. Joy, I am so sorry!" She reached to squeeze her friend's hand. "I know you will survive, and things will get better for you and Jules."

"I hate the man with a passion!" Joy said. "But there's not one thing I can or would do about it. I might speak to him when hell freezes over. I don't want Jules to ever know I made these remarks. It would just hurt her." Joy took a deep breath. "Now my best friends know, and there is no reason to talk about it again." She waved her hand in the air. "It's history, done, over. Let's move forward."

Jettie reached out and squeezed Joy's hand for the second time. "I'm sorry, honey, and I'm sick for Jules."

Joy thanked them for being there, as they always had been. "I do have one thing to ask ya'll, and then I'm finished. I have to know. It's bugged me a long time. What's wrong with me? First, I lost Vince to another girl. Then I lost Frank, not even aware it was to another family. Why does that happen to me? What am I doing wrong?"

Jettie pointed her finger in Joy's face. "Joy, don't even go there. It's not you. You're a wonderful woman; he screwed up, not you. You have crappy luck and you deserve better. Plus, we love you. Who gives a damn if he doesn't?"

Dixie chimed in her chipper voice, "That's exactly right, and you never know who's right around the corner, missy."

Joy's face relaxed. "Well, you can bet your last dollar, sister, that I'll be on the look out. I don't intend to spend the rest of my days alone, no offense." She pushed the shredded napkin aside and pulled her shoulders back. "Now, ladies, get out your day-timers and let's make sure we're all on the same page. We have things to do, people to see, places to go and parties to plan."

"I wonder what Vince is doing now?" Jettie asked. Vince had been Joy's sweetheart in high school.

"I don't know," Joy said. "But I'd love to find out."

Jettie smiled. "I'll bet you would."

Life was almost back to normal. Laughter tinkled in the air. Joy thumbed through her day-timer. "Be sure and mark your calendars for our fortieth Silver Springs High School Reunion."

"Oh my gosh." Jettie's eyes looked as big as Betty Boop's. "When is it? That's been the furthest thing from my mind."

"It's in three months. All of the old gang is supposed to be there. Do you have a problem?"

Dixie smacked her freshly-applied ruby red lips. "Not me, count me in." She snapped her compact together. "I'll be there with bells on!"

Jettie thumbed through her calendar. "It's just that our Las Vegas trip is . . ." She turned another page. "Ah, never mind. That trip is next month, and we'll be back in plenty of time."

Dixie looked at Joy, then at Jettie. "What's this about a Vegas trip?"

Jettie smiled and closed her day-timer. "Girl, I thought I told you about Toby's invitation to play on the Texas Hold-Em Poker Tournament on television. This tournament has been his lifetime dream. He has all the plans together; he'll be behind the wheel of his love—the motor coach—and says we will be gone for one week."

Dixie closed her day-timer. "I can't believe you're going to Vegas. I never have time to go to the casinos in Louisiana, just 120 miles away."

"I plan on being right there, cheering him on. Besides, my slot arm will need a rest." Jettie raised her arm and pulled on an invisible handle. "I hope it's worn out from the heavy buckets of money I have to carry."

"Okay," Joy said, "ladies, let's return from our trips and back to the reunion."

Jettie cleared her throat and used her hand to make a zip-like motion across her lips. "Okay, madam; carry on."

"Being a planner on the committee has given me an inside track on information, and I understand there will be more returnee students this year than ever in our history."

"Woo Hoo." Dixie May cheered and clapped her hands. "I can't wait to see those stud muffin jocks. I bet every one of them is fat and bald. They probably follow their little women around, real Mr. Universes."

Jettie almost spit her tea on the table when Dixie made that statement. They all roared with laughter.

It was just the medicine Joy needed after her run of bad news.

Jettie gained her composure. "About attendees, Joy. Is he going to be there, hmm?"

Joy gave Jettie the look. They all knew the look and what it meant. Joy smiled, then squealed with delight. "Yes, one of the other committee helpers received Vince's RSVP, and he's coming!"

Dixie said, "Hot damn! That cutie is one that's never made it back. I can't wait to see him. How about you, Joy?" Joy smiled at Dixie but said nothing.

Jettie added, "Well, is his wife's name on the RSVP?"

Joy answered, "We're not privy to that information. But it will be just wonderful to see him after all these years, even if his wife attends. Forty years; what do you expect? I hope he's not the Mr. Universe type Dixie May described." Laughter thundered.

"Jot this down," Joy ordered. "The reunion is on May fifteenth at the Fairmont Hotel in Dallas, in the Grand Elite Ballroom. Six o'clock cocktails and dinner at seven. Mr. Marsh has planned an enchanted night to remember; the program will be fabulous. It promises to be the largest reunion ever, so be sure and reserve a room so we can all eat breakfast together at the hotel the next morning."

Joy smiled at Dixie and batted her eyelashes. "Dixie May, I have a special favor to ask, girlfriend."

Dixie raised an eyebrow. "Uh-oh. Anything for you, darling."

"Well, you know how picky I am when it comes to my looks. I want you to do a complete makeover on me, and I promise not to interfere." She held up her hands and shook her head. "I want to look my best, and when we rate all the oldies but goodies with our 10 x magnifier and a critique sheet, I definitely want to be measured as a ten."

They high-fived each other.

"You are the best!" Joy said, and gave her the thumbs up sign.

Jettie, not to be out done, wedged in with, "Joy's not to get ahead of me. I want a make-over too!" She instructed Dixie May, "Jot it down." Jettie raised her glass. "Let's make a toast." They clicked glasses, and Jettie announced, "Heart-to-heart forever."

Dixie May jumped up. "Maybe ya'll better consider an upgrade to a full blown facelift." She turned on her high heel slings and prissed her tiny hiney off to the ladies room, where they could hear her cute giggle as she rounded the corner. The friends had made a vow years ago never to grow old before their time. It was the unspoken law of the sisterhood. Dixie May told them she had seen so many attractive women allow others to dictate what they should look or dress like, and they had turned into old women, like they had no ideas or will of their own. The girlfriends were a unique group of ladies, and not one of them wanted to become an old woman over night. They had younger minds, even though their bodies had aged. They planned to live and enjoy life for as long as they were physically able. Joy had said many times over the years, "Young people do not have a patent on youth and love of music or life; nobody should make you feel old until you are ready."

The food arrived. The Trio Salad Combo made a beautiful presentation with chunky white chicken salad on leafy romaine lettuce. Chopped pecans and sliced purple grapes garnished the top. A tropical fruit salad with a delicate slice of banana nut bread and corkscrew pasta salad completed the Trio. Dixie asked Marie to take a picture of her and her girlfriends.

When finished, Jettie cleared her throat, took her knife and tapped the side of her water goblet. "Okay, ladies. It's been brought to my attention that Dixie May has a new beau, and we want the details."

This announcement started a chain reaction. Joy leaned on the table with one elbow and said with exaggerated emphasis, "Details, please, ma'am."

Dixie May decided to be the drama queen. "Why, yes, do I ever. It's like this . . ." She fluttered her hands about, and shook one hand like it was hot. "Well, about three weeks ago this tall cool drink of water walked into my shop in search of the best haircut in town."

"Hhmmm, and?" Joy said.

"He was handsome and sexy. He sauntered over to my station and said, 'I need a haircut. A local yokel told me that a gal named Dixie May was the one to see.' I said, 'You got lucky.' He stood there a minute, then said, 'Is that you?' I said, 'In the flesh. Have a seat and I'll be right with you as soon as I finish this haircut.' He did."

"Then what?" Jettie asked.

"After I put my mojo on him, he's been a shadow on my doorstep ever since. We closed the shop and had a hamburger that night. At present, we've been on a total of ten dates."

"My, my. So, more details, please." Joy rubbed lotion on her hands and forearms. She offered the lotion. "Anyone else dry as me?"

"He has many interests; movies, dinners, and slow dances are our specialty." Jettie and Joy were spellbound as they sat and hung on every word Dixie spoke. She hadn't had this kind of interest in any man in the last twelve years. "Please note he's a fine dancer, ladies; you know I like that. Oh, yeah!"

"So, who is this guy and where did he come from?" Joy replaced the lotion in her bag, which she replaced on the back of her chair.

"Oh, he's a hotshot. On the serious side, he's an engineer who designs large buildings and convention centers, specializes in critical situations. When the local talent can't handle the job, they fly him in. He could be here a year; it all depends on how the hotel plans come together in Greenville."

Jettie and Joy exchanged looks. They were well in tune to how special Dixie thought this man was.

Gideon, the manager, stopped at their table. He carried a bottle of Chardonnay. "More wine, ladies?"

Dixie laughed. "No thanks. I'm on a natural high and have a long way to drive."

He smiled. "Where's Mrs. Barrett today?"

Joy answered, "Now, Gideon, you know Krystal. She and Johnny make time for more romantic rendezvous than anybody we've ever known. They have made the effort to keep romance alive until this very day, and that's a fact, Jack."

Dixie May stood up with her hands on her hips. "Sisters, can I have an amen?"

All the girls said, "Amen." Krystal was a close friend to the clique of friends, but she spent most of her spare time with her husband. She was a tall blonde and always had her agenda booked. She and Johnny were made for each other—he was tall and thin and they made an excellent couple. Whatever he did, she supported, whether it was riding the Harley, sailing, dinner, dancing, movies, or simply making a plan to be together. They loved to dress up, and above all else, work romance into their lives.

Gideon half smiled and told them to stay out of trouble.

Jettie made a mental note to call and fill Krystal in on Joy and Frank.

Joy cleared her throat. "Ladies, please, I'm not finished. Dixie May, tell me, does this beau have a brother?"

Jettie chimed in, fanning her hands in the air, "Hey, when do we get to meet this incredible find?"

Dixie said, "Girls, let me answer one question at a time. Mercy!"

She shook her head and grumbled. "I haven't been interrogated like since my first car date, and that poor guy had to go through my daddy. Now back to the man. No brother, Joy! He's a rare find. And you ladies can drool all over yourselves when I have him stop by the salon on ya'll's day of beauty!"

"All right!" Jettie popped off. "We get a private showing. Now, that's a plan!" They jotted in their day planners the dates for the reunion and the day of beauty. Marie walked to their table, but before she left the check, she said, "Ya'll are so much fun you make our day, so do it more often."

Jettie shifted in her chair and looked directly into Dixie May's eyes. "Okay now, wait a minute. I have an important question: how is Mr. Cool in the kissy department? That's at the top of my list." Jettie didn't even slow down. "If they can't work up a good pucker, sucker, then I'm not interested. I cut them from the herd." Not letting anyone get a word in, Jettie continued, determined to make her point. "I think I was marked by that date with that donut kisser that Joy stuck me with years ago. Remember him, Joy?" The accuser stared at Joy, still miffed after all these years.

Joy answered, "You've never let me live it down." She hung her head in her hands.

"Why, I won't ever forget that awful blind date, my first and last, when Joy begged me to go with this guy so she could see Vince. What you do for friends." Jettie pretended to smack her palm to her forehead. "Vince didn't have a car yet, and her parents wouldn't allow Joy to go alone with the two guys. This guy, Reggie, had a hot '58 black Impala convertible. It was the fastest, most gorgeous car in town. It was lowered all the way around and 'Crawling Crab' was written on the rear fender. It smoked everybody out at the Red Hill Drag Strip, remember, Joy?"

Joy nodded and said, "Oh yes, girl, do I ever. We were sixteen and dying to be twenty-one."

Jettie continued, "The car was cool, but this square kissed like a donut, I swear. He'd make this big hard circle with his lips—" She demonstrated as she talked. "—and it had a hole in the middle when he kissed you. It felt like a big old hard donut pressed against my mouth. Why, I had no idea what to do with it. I didn't know if I should try to make my lips like a donut or stick my tongue in that hole. I didn't know if I was to send or receive."

The girls laughed tears by then.

"It reminded you of some of those pictures of a big old swollen hemorrhoid. It was awful. I never kissed anyone like him before or since."

They gasped for air, more laughter and tears.

"Well, Miss Joy, I guess you remember when I faked sick so I could go home?"

"Uh, yeah, Jettie. That was the longest night of my life."

"Well, ol' Reggie didn't let me off that easy. Oh, no." She shook her head. "When we pulled up in front of my house, he jumped out on his side and rushed around to my side to walk me to the door. I remember when I looked back over my shoulder at Joy, she knew what that look meant." Jettie gave the look to Joy.

"I knew I'd never hear the end of it," Joy said. "Exhibit A, forty years later." She rolled her hand palm up, indicating the moment.

"Well, he couldn't wait to get me to that door to slip me the donut one more time. It took everything in me not to laugh in his face or bolt in and slam my door. Didn't ya'll hear me scream in laughter inside the door?"

A burst of fresh giggles filled the room. Joy laughed so hard her sides hurt. No doubt the tearoom folks would think they were drunk!

Dixie May gasped, then squeaked, "You're lying. Who was this guy? What happened to him?" Dixie fanned her hot cheeks with both hands,

Jettie exclaimed, "Oh girl, he still lives here, he and his family. He is Pastor David down at the Little Elm Baptist Church. You know he and his wife have six kids." She blew her nose and wiped her eyes.

"Ya'll hush, you're about to make me wet my pants." Joy scooted out of her chair and stood to leave. "They're looking at us; we better get out of here. They might tell us to never come back."

They grabbed their purses and scrambled to the door much like silly teenagers. Dixie May told them in the parking lot, "Whew…they say when you laugh, you release endorphins and it's good for your stress level, so we should be in great shape! And, hold it, I want a picture." Afterwards they hugged goodbye until the next heart-to-heart, and got in their cars. The friends pulled out of the lot single file, then scattered like the wind.

Jettie pulled onto the interstate, her mind full of the day's events. Here at their age, they were still able to let it all hang out and be silly for a while, their cares to the side as they laughed and chased away the blues. As Jettie's mother used to say, "It's better to laugh than cry." She was glad that Joy had called them together to bare her soul, and she was glad to hear Joy say, "Let's move on." All the laughs were healing. And, Jettie was so happy for Dixie May. She headed east with her pedal pressed to the metal, anxious to see her man. It made her heart sing to hear Dixie May say, "My knight has arrived to whisk me away." The perky little redhead had people to see, places to go and things to do. That pleased Jettie.

Chapter 4

For the McNamaras to be away for a week took lots of planning. Toby had to get the coach serviced, then make reservations for the special events they wanted to attend in Vegas. Jettie had people coming to change the televisions throughout their home to HD flat screens. It would be nice when they returned for Toby to watch Hold-Em on the big screen. The installation of a gazebo was also on their agenda.

The big day finally arrived. Viva Las Vegas. They were on their way. The Dallas skyline was behind them as they headed west.

Miss Personality was the name she'd always been referred to her entire life, the belle of the ball, the center of attention. Jettie was deep in thought as she lay on the bed of the forty-five-foot luxury coach. This was their third motor home, and it was used for all their business and most of their pleasure trips. They tooled down the highway at a comfortable pace on cruise control.

Toby sat behind the wheel of his pride and joy; no place would he rather be, other than a poker table. Some people had their golf, but Toby had his poker. He was a true workaholic, and, well, maybe a pokerholic. The only time he relaxed was when he did one of those two things.

It was here that Jettie could rest, with no phones or interruptions. Here in the confines of this oasis on wheels was where Jettie hid out and dreamed and reflected. Today it was her past that settled into her psyche. Thoughts of years gone by. As gabby as Jettie was, the one thing that was never up for discussion was her early years. Outside of the sessions with her friends, this was where the friendly, personable, extroverted yet private person sought her solitude to regenerate and get her priorities in order.

Her early childhood had been a dysfunctional mess. With an abusive, alcoholic father, Jettie lived a life of hardship, deprived of basic needs. She and Joy talked many times and agreed that their friendship saved Jettie. It kept her off the shrink's couch. And their close bond of girly-girl talks had certainly given birth to the "heart-to-heart" sessions her friends now held whenever possible. She and Joy had shared a lifetime of woes and wins, and they would always understand each other, although they would not always agree. They had an unconditional love; they knew the good, bad and the ugly about each other, and they accepted it all. These true soul sisters would never share private information outside their twosome. They honored each other's privacy and their word was never questioned.

Jettie remembered the first time she met Joy. They were in eighth grade. Even then, Jettie and Joy were totally different. Jettie had several friends that attended ballgames and church events, but she and Joy were friends solely between the two of them. They met and lived in Dallas before Jettie's family moved to Silver Springs. Joy's family returned to their hometown in the country, just a few miles out of Silver Springs, where the girls continued in school. They wanted to spend a great deal of time together, and Joy's daddy would take them to the movies and drop them off. Other times, her mom and dad liked to fish, and they would tag along and have to stay all day. Jettie remembered the day Joy wore short shorts, and her daddy made her change into longer pants. He was a wonderful father figure, and Jettie always enjoyed Joy's family. They never grew tired of one another, but wanted to spend every minute together. Her family was opposite of Jettie's. Unlike Jettie's, Joy's parents were still married. That was when marriages lasted forever.

Jettie's mother, Judith, met and fell in love with her father, Jennings, also a country boy, but as wild as the wind.

Jennings told his mother, "I have found a little girl to marry, and I can raise her like I want her." Judith had lost her own mother when she was nine and just fell in love with Martha, Jennings mother. Judith became his teen bride. They lived close to his family. Their first child was a boy, and he was loved by many. When it came time for his haircut, it was a big event; children were rare in this family. His mother, daddy, grandfather and grandmother, aunt and uncles came and they all went to the barber shop to see him get his hair cut. That is how close this family was. Martha took Judith under her wing and taught her to cook fried chicken, banana pudding and biscuits, Jennings' favorites.

Sadly, Judith was victimized; Jennings was an abuser. The ten-year marriage produced two beautiful blue-eyed children, Wayne and Jettie, but that is where the beauty ended. The goal was to survive. Jennings became deadly, and not only did Judith suffer from his fists, but so did their fragile asthmatic son. Jettie only experienced one belt whipping from her daddy, and it was delivered with brutality. Jennings beat Judith as if she were a man. The children were horrified. The sound of knuckles tearing flesh, followed by whimpers and wails filled them with hopelessness and fear. They crouched and prayed to escape the violence.

Jettie's mother sought help. The police were a joke. They turned their backs and left the victims to be attacked before they left the driveway. Jettie, even as a young child, knew that it was wrong. She resented the callous way the police responded to violence on women and children, leaving them utterly defenseless. It was disgraceful and inhumane. She thought it odd that her daddy was such a sweet and good man when he was sober and a crazy man when he drank. One night when he was on a tear, they hid in the bushes, out away from their home in a field. He called to them. They were afraid to breathe, dared not make a peep. It was horrific, but the next day, it was like it had never happened. Jettie's father would be normal, showed love and kindness. It boggled Jettie's mind. The normalcy lasted until he got liquored up again, which was often.

Time after torturous time she heard the sound of her father's belt slicing through the air and cutting into her brother's tender flesh. She felt the burn as if she were the one being beaten. She heard Wayne whimper, but they were her own whimpers. She was afraid to scream, afraid Daddy might get worse. Whack by endless whack, she reeled as she experienced the pain of the lick. Wayne's small body yielded to each impact and trembled in sheer terror.

No one knows what goes through children's minds when they live in that hell. They don't know where and when it is going to end. They are helpless and have no place to hide, no place to go, no place to flee for safety. Only when they were alone did they comfort and cuddle, like two tiny puppies that licked each other's wounds.

They did their best to soothe the other's pain away.

Filled with confusion, Jettie imagined her daddy like the movie character, Dr. Jeckle and Mr. Hyde. She and Wayne spent hours at the movies, mesmerized by the film. In all honesty, it was their escape. Even as very young children, they were able to stay all day, sit through a double feature, cartoons and the newsreels. There they could feel the comfort of the dark theatre where they were swept away to a beautiful and happy place. To a place where all people were heroes and kind to each other.

Jettie remembered the Saturday matinees and all the time she spent with her brother. He had a habit of sucking his thumb, and at the same time he would rub her toes. Those two things went hand in hand. She'd observed other thumb suckers and noticed they usually had a dual habit that went along with the thumb sucking, like feeling a corner of a blanket or pillow. She smiled, understanding that had been his way of feeling secure, to feel Sissy's toes and suck security right out of his thumb. They lived through the indescribable insanity that no child should be expected to witness.

Her mother managed to escape that marriage from hell. Jettie's mother remarried after five years of single life. It was tough, with no car, to make a living for two children. She walked them to school and then walked to work and back every day, rain, shine, sleet or snow. The kids enjoyed having her all to themselves. But, it would not last. The new husband was a good provider and did not physically hurt her mother or the children, but he was jealous of Jettie. He played mind games. He deprived her and made her feel unworthy by giving his sons an allowance while neglecting to give her one as well. She was never allowed to drive the family car. She loved her home when he wasn't there, but when he was, she felt he begrudged every bite she put in her mouth. She felt that way the entire time she lived with them. She tolerated him from ages nine to eighteen. He had children of his own, and he intended for Judith to raise them. Jettie would never receive the love and attention she needed. She would inevitably end up as the caboose in a long line of children and her stepfather's needs. She would never forgive her stepfather for his selfishness and his ability to block her from her mother. Jettie resented her mother for allowing that to happen.

Jettie survived and thrived as she grew older. However, it took a lifetime for her to come to terms with her Cinderella life, unfulfilled needs, and resentment for the pain she and her brother were forced to endure. Wayne lost his will to live at a young thirty-eight and decided to end his torment. Jettie was thirty-six when he aimed a shotgun at his heart and ended his young life. She mourned him and felt deep resentment that he had been sacrificed. She blamed everyone that had allowed this to happen. He had never been able to pull out of the grave that had been dug for him as a youngster. He could never find his way to live normally; he was too screwed up. Yet to look at him, you saw a gorgeous man who women migrated to and couldn't get enough of. Year after year, she watched as it became increasingly more difficult for him to cope, never understanding why he followed his father's footsteps, sucked to the bottom of a beer bottle. She hated her daddy for the pain and anguish he brought down on his family. Later she would harbor anger against her stepfather, as well, and blame her mother for allowing it to happen again.

Later Jettie became consumed with researching mental illness. She was convinced that her dad had been manic-depressive and died too young to benefit from the drugs that would become available in the next decade.

At last Jettie made peace with the past and forgave her father. No longer devoured by anger, she was able to understand that he'd been a victim of his own demons. Twenty years earlier, Jettie had accepted Christ. She craved His love and awoke every glorious morning praising Him and giving thanks for another opportunity to live for Him.

Jettie rose from the bed and straightened her clothes, not as rested as she might have been had the ghosts of her past not visited her today. She felt in harmony.

Careful not to fall, she made her way to the front of the coach, guiding herself as the mighty bus roared down life's highway for another adventure. Toby saw her in the mirror. She leaned down and planted a big kiss on his cheek and told him how much she loved him. "Daddy, where are we going to eat?"

They would make Albuquerque by nightfall, then drive all day tomorrow, when they would pull into the RV Park at Circus Circus.

It was time to run and play—to make new memories in their favorite city that never slept. She loved to admire the beautiful Nevada skies, with all the billions of lights that would guide their way to Caesar's Palace. "Daddy," as she called Toby, would sit behind the poker table. He was in his element, doing his thing, and she was glad. A good, hard-working man, Toby had earned his time to play.

She remarked to a friend, "If Toby wants me to sit on a stool next to him while he plays poker, I will do it 'til the world is flat, if it will make him happy. After all, a great man is hard to find and harder to keep."

Jettie put all thoughts of the past and home behind her as she joined Toby after he unhooked from the bus. They got in their car and headed toward the strip. He wasn't scheduled to play in the tournament until tomorrow noon, and tonight was their night to run and play.

Chapter 5

Work, work, work! It was Saturday and Dixie was at the shop. She'd had a great week. Her entire life centered on the salon and Chet. She thought of him and the life they could have. She could easily daydream and do hair—almost with her eyes closed, she'd been doing it so long. She wondered what their future might be. He spoke of California and its beauty. She could relate, although she'd only been to San Francisco once to a hair show with some friends in the business. They shared a room and toured the city. The coast was magnificent; she knew how people could relate to Tony Bennett singing the incredible "I Left My Heart in San Francisco." It was the primo romantic city. But, that's all she'd seen of the city and the state.

Many times Chet mentioned the beaches, Fisherman Wharf and the wineries. She guessed he was a little homesick for the hustle and bustle of the city by the sea. It was a world away from Silver Springs. But, Chet said he loved quaint little Chapel Valley, with its courthouse on the square and small town atmosphere where everybody seemed to know everybody else. He was crazy about Wednesday night's all-you-could-eat catfish at Lake Fork. Nothing interfered with that dinner plan.

In many ways their routine was similar to that of married people, which Dixie had been a time or two. She'd been there and done that and dated a lot of men. She'd experienced pain on numerous occasions. She'd heard the alarm go off as a warning in her brain, but she blew caution to the wind. She'd let her defenses down with this guy. She trusted him. In years past she had experienced the loneliness and the gnawing emptiness once a love affair was over. She tried to pace herself and keep a distance between her and Chet, but she was so happy with their relationship, she eased up on the boundaries. He seemed to only have eyes for her. She saw plenty of single women checking him out when they danced; clearly they were intrigued with his good looks and sexy manner.

Jettie arrived early at the store, needing to catch up since they had just returned from the Vegas trip. "We had to come home to get some rest," Jettie told some of the customers. "We had such a great time, as usual. Toby placed in the top twenty players, which was great, considering there were thousands when it all started months ago."

She had an ad deadline that had to be completed and signed off on. Her secretary announced that Krystal was on line one. She didn't have the time to spare, but Krystal was a friend and she would make it brief. Krystal was excited about the fortieth reunion. They chatted about fifteen minutes, and Jettie took the time to fill her in on some of the girly gossip. "Okay, so tell me what you are going to wear," Krystal said.

"Let me see," Jettie said. "I'll run it down to the smallest detail. I bought a special outfit in Vegas, so I'll be dressed for comfort and the look. It's an Oriental, after-five black party pants with a matching sheer, long sleeve jacket that flows to mid calf and splits up the sides. My shoes are mid-heel slings. My hair will be up and decorated with a pair of oriental chopsticks. Now, how is that for detail?"

"I can always count on you to have it all together, Miss Jettie. I'm not for sure what I'll decide, but I'm getting a plan together, now that we're off the road awhile. I'll talk to you soon."

On Thursday morning, Jettie picked Dixie up and they drove to Chapel Valley—a scenic forty miles from Silver Springs—to arrive by ten a.m.

They had allowed time for a long day of hair coloring, haircuts, facials, pedicures and manicures. Lunch would be delivered by the Lunch Basket, a unique concept where a young girl delivered the delicacies. Their gourmet sandwiches, spritzer drinks, and variety of fresh cut fruit placed amongst an array of homemade cookies were presented in a lovely wicker basket covered with a checkered cloth. The ladies delighted in the small town service. They used it every opportunity they had.

Joy was first in the chair, draped and ready to become a new woman under the magic touch and direction of Dixie May, who mixed the color and staged everything she would need, including the little bowls and brushes. This was a major undertaking. Joy was about 80% gray, and her friends had talked to her forever to make a change. But she balked, and it never happened. Well, today was different. She was in Dixie's chair. Jettie, not wanting to miss a detail, sat in the next salon chair. But she was busy flipping pages in a magazine in search of a new style. Dixie sectioned Joy's hair into thin sections and applied different shades of color to the hair that rested on a strip of foil. As each piece was brushed with color, she folded the foil up and repeated the process over Joy's entire head. Dixie turned on the timer for twenty minutes. Brave Joy sat in the chair but kept her mouth shut, even though the thought of bolting and ripping the foil sections from her hair was overwhelming. She felt like yelling, "Yikes, forget it, I've changed my mind."

Joy marveled at how expertly and fast Dixie worked. "Well, this isn't too bad," she said aloud.

Trudy showed up beside Joy. "Come this way."

Joy slipped out of the chair and followed her to the other side of the room to a large platform where she crawled up into a big chair. Trudy rolled up Joy's pant legs to the knee and placed her feet in a tub of warm water. The chair massaged her back and buttocks while the whirlpool softened and soaked her feet.

"Goodness, this is good," Joy said. "Look at what I've been missing."

Trudy continued to run water and add solution to the foot bath as she organized her pedicure tools and straddled the stool by Joy's feet. Joy was stretched out full length in the large chair with her eyes closed when she felt someone on her right. She opened one eye as Star placed her hand in a warm solution to soak and soften before grooming. She left Joy's hand covered with a towel, never said a word, then walked away. Joy wasn't one to hang out at the beauty shop, but she began to catch on to the routine: it all targeted relaxation. She needed to hang in the beauty shop more often; then she could cut down on Dr. Avery appointments.

Dixie mixed color in a bowl with a brush, swirled it around to make a paste, then painted Jettie's new growth, which was naturally brunette and had never developed gray like her peers. She preferred blond, as did her husband. Today she would get a touch up, and Dixie would trim her ends. She trusted Dixie, she had always taken care of her and nobody knew it better.

Joy's new color unfolded as each piece of the foil was removed. Dixie exclaimed," Oh my! Girls, I knew I was right. It's better than I thought it would be; look at her eyes. "

Dixie turned the chair around to face the mirror. "So—what do you think? Not just your eyes, but your entire face is enhanced by this color. And, it will get even better when it's shampooed and styled."

"Girls, I have to admit, I like what I see," Joy said. "So far, that is."

After Trudy shampooed the color from Jettie's hair and wrapped her with conditioner, the Lunch Basket arrived. The delivery girl collected money from everyone, then left the goodies on the table. Dixie had arranged a covered table especially for their special day. Star arranged the food, then gathered plates and forks. The girls served themselves buffet style. The operators took their lunches and sat in the middle of the salon with the two ladies wearing foil strips on their head. It was so much fun; there was no place like a small town beauty shop. It resembled children dressing up and hosting tea parties. The operators had scheduled their appointments well, allowing for the break in their schedules. Dixie had not booked anyone else; she intended to dedicate her day to her friends and their day of beauty, and she didn't want to miss one second of it.

Joy licked her lips. "This food is delish. I wish they did this in Silver Springs."

"Oh, the people around here are spoiled and may not even think it is special or unusual," Dixie said

"Not special, my foot," Jettie said. "If they had to drive to pick up food everyday like we do, they'd appreciate it."

Trudy was fun and happy to join in. She seemed to enjoy the camaraderie of the women. But Star was peculiar and did just the opposite—she was a strange bird.

The food was eaten right down to the last few grapes and one lone strawberry. "What a bunch of pigs!" Dixie teased. The timing was perfect. Joy and Jettie's feet and hands were finished, their hair had been colored and shampooed, and they were wrapped in towels. Next would be the facials and the grand finale—the unveiling of Joy's new hairstyle.

"It's back to the drawing board," Dixie said. Trudy motioned Jettie into the facial room, and Dixie took Joy to the styling chair. The shears flew as Dixie nipped and snipped hair that piled on her mat. Joy was wide eyed but didn't utter a word.

Dixie locked eyes with her in the mirror. "Joy, you look like a frightened child. It's all right." She whirled the chair around so Joy could no longer see.

"Now, Dixie May, that's not fair!" Joy squealed.

Dixie laughed. "Well, girl, I never said it would be."

Joy was trapped with a drape over her shoulders. She sat—unable to move. All she needed was a seat belt and she would have felt like she was strapped in at the county fair for the most dangerous ride she had ever experienced. Her big eyes were the doorway to the brain, and Dixie could see the wheels turning.

Well, Joy had a plan. As soon as Dixie let up on those scissors, she would jump up and grab the mirror to get a gander all the way around. "Dixie May," she blurted out, "you're enjoying this way too much."

Dixie smiled while she pumped the chair up with her foot. "I can't deny that."

The snipping stopped. Joy felt a draft on the back of her neck. Dixie grabbed the big airbrush and snapped the blower into place and blew and wrapped Joy's hair with lightening speed. She deliberately kept the chair turned backwards, not allowing Joy to see until she was finished.

The attention made Joy sleepy; it would be easy to drift off. The chair whirled; Joy was face to face with a new woman—wow!

Dixie snapped the drape from Joy's shoulders. "Now what do you think?"

Joy grabbed the mirror. Her straight, shiny hair had slivers of dark brunette and two different shades of blond—one was gold, the other a pale baby blond. She was pleased! Joy bounced from the chair. "Dixie May, you are one talented woman." She kissed her on the cheek. "Thanks for making me so beautiful." She took off to the facial room and swung open the door. "Jettie, look at me!"

With that, Jettie opened her eyes and gasped. "Why, girl, it's gorgeous, just like I knew it would be."

Trudy had finished with Jettie. They walked to Dixie's station. Jettie patted Dixie on the shoulder. "Girl, you did a fantastic job, as I knew you would. Our friend looks twenty years younger. Okay, Dixie May, crank up the talent; it's my turn."

Joy headed into the facial room. Jettie's hair turned out great. They were born-again women, only in a different sense.

As they gathered their goodies to leave, Chet walked in. Dixie introduced everyone and they all shook hands. They talked a bit, then the ladies had to leave. Dixie and Chet made a cute couple; he had walked over and gave her a hug; it was apparent that it made her day. Jettie made a point to invite them to the country for steaks. Chet said, "I'll hold you to it." She had an ulterior motive; she wanted to get to know him a little better. There was an unsettled feeling she had about him, and she could better put her finger on it once she spent a little time with him. But she did observe Dixie May light up like a Christmas tree when he walked in. When he wasn't looking, the girls gave her their thumbs up approval and left. Dixie May blew them a kiss and got back to her man.

Chapter 6

Jules was crazy about her mom's new youthful look. The next step was the shopping mall for the reunion dress. She wanted to help her mom pick out everything for this exciting time in her life. And number one, Jules wanted her mom to feel as good as she possibly could about herself and find a new beginning in her life. She wanted her mother's life back on track so she could be as happy as Jules was.

Joy kept busy and dealt with the Frank situation. The one wonderful thing she knew and kept to herself, Frank would not be coming to the reunion. What a relief. She would not want to deal with him and his new woman, not at this reunion. The sale of the house was well on the way. The lawyers determined that Frank should buy Joy out, and he could remain as owner. She didn't care. Any happy memories she had of the twenty-nine year marriage had been squashed with one look at that photo.

The weeks flew off the calendar. The closer the date of the reunion, the more excited Jettie and Joy became. They just felt this one was going to be special, unlike any reunion they had ever celebrated in the past.

Joy asked, "Girl, do you think it's our age?" She and Jettie often got in the car and rode to town and checked out new areas and old areas. They discussed how the town had changed. On occasion, they would grab a sack lunch, go to the city park, and sit in their car while they ate and watched the people walk or feed the ducks. There was always an activity to be enjoyed. Both would speak of their families and the old days and their youth. It was marvelous to know someone so well and have so many memories to remember and discuss.

Jettie couldn't wait to get to the hotel early so she could visit with some of her old classmates from her homemaking class: Anita, Barbara, Donna and Janice. Several lived locally, so they talked on occasion or even met up in the grocery store and spent a lot of time visiting in the produce section. Jettie enjoyed school and all the friends.

Several girls from her homemaking class were always around. They had lots to remember from their home-ec days in Mrs. Barclay's class. "She was such a mean old woman," Jettie grumbled, "I won't ever forget her tearing out the entire apron my mother sewed for me. I was desperate and wasn't able to make the old bat happy with any of my efforts, so Mother made it and I turned it in. Then Mrs. Barclay tore out every stitch. Mother was hopping mad!"

One of the classmates hadn't returned since their tenth year reunion. She was now a televised celebrity on a food show, The Dining Diva. Her real name was Smitti Parker. The ladies wanted to quiz her. They were curious because Smitti spent most of her time in the girl's restroom smoking and was the worst student in history. So, when in the world did she learn to cook?

Reunion day arrived. At the hotel, Jettie signed in and tagged while Joy greeted the classmates. The ballroom was decorated in the style of the '50s, and excitement filled the air. Jettie, Toby, Dixie, Chet, Krystal, and Johnny were seated at Joy's table. Since Joy served as an organizer, she received additional perks, such as a front table close to the band and the entrance. Plus a free ticket to the reunion and two free passes to Jazz in the Park on Saturday evening.

Joy told Jettie a few days before the big night, "Jules was more excited about the reunion than me. She insisted that I buy a special dress to go with my new makeover."

Jettie had said, "That is so sweet. Daughter taking care of her mama."

"We made the most of our time together. After trying a dozen dresses, Jules selected this one."

"Mercy, she has good taste, girlfriend." Jettie felt the fabric and nodded in approval.

"To help me get in the spirit of the occasion, I decided to wear this old locket."

Jettie moved in for a closer look; it was dainty, just like Joy.

"Remember? It's the one Vince gave me. I thought it would help get me in the spirit of the party." The locket still had both of their photos inside; she was radiant that evening in May. It was obvious she was full of confidence with her new look.

Jettie was happy to see the old Joy resurface after being down for weeks.

The reunion kicked off at six with cocktails, dinner was served at seven, and by eight-thirty, a crowd packed the polished dance floor. High school memorabilia covered the tables and walls and a mascot in a tiger suit paraded through the ballroom. It was a hoot to see a tall tiger holding his tail as he danced in the spotlight with the principal's wife.

Wide screen monitors displayed in the corners of the ballroom enhanced memories as they displayed school events, pep rallies, football games, plays, band concerts, graduation, and photos of the kids back in their days at Central High.

"It's a hoot," Krystal told a few of the girls she knew from her drama class. "What an outstanding job the committee had done!" That was the buzz in the crowd.

Krystal and Johnny were among the first guests to arrive. They weren't strangers to the band, who were dressed like crooners from the era.

Toby sat at the table while Jettie stood close to registration, but she was within ear shot. Toby said, "That old Johnny is a smooth operator; look at them on the floor."

Jettie said, "Love, they would rather dance than eat. See how skinny they are?"

The waitresses, decked out in black polka dot short shorts and pink blouses, with ponytails tied with black scarves, served drinks. The crooners crooned and the back-up girls sang harmony. The girls wore full petticoats and poodle skirts. The staging worked; they felt like they were in the '50s.

They belted out the lyrics of "School Days." Although Joy was engrossed in the entertainment, a feeling made her turn to see a man signing in. She hadn't seen his face when he entered, but now he was leaning over. She poked Jettie. "I think that's Vince. Can you believe that's him?"

Jettie looked. "I think you're right." She shoved her slightly. "Go greet him."

Joy, cheeks a little flushed, rose from the chair, mustered up a big smile, walked up behind him and said, "Vince Chandler, is that you?"

He turned. The man, tanned a golden brown with twinkling blue eyes and sun-kissed blond hair, was even more handsome than she remembered. Their eyes locked. "Joy."

Without hesitation, they reached for each other. Joy pulled back, although their hands still joined, and said, "It's so good to see you after all these years." She looked behind him, over his shoulder.

He followed her gaze and also looked behind him, with a question in his face.

"Introduce me to Mrs. Chandler."

He lowered his head, then raised it again, pain clearly showing on his face. "I lost Cricket and our two sons in a car wreck three years ago."

Shocked and deeply saddened by his horrible loss, Joy uttered a feeble, "I'm so sorry." She felt the need to lean into him and hold him; they embraced. Regaining her composure, she pulled away, yet kept his right hand in hers. "Come on; let's see if you'll recognize any of the old gang."

As they started to walk, he stopped. "Is that the locket?"

She touched it and nodded. "It helped me get into a nostalgic mood for this evening."

He reached in his pocket and pulled out a key ring. It displayed photos of them. "Joy, we always did think alike." Still holding hands, he turned hers over. "What about you?"

"We divorced two years ago. I have a daughter, Jules." She led Vince to the table where Jettie and Dixie were seated, and they all greeted him. Dixie introduced Chet. Vince was invited to join their table; he accepted.

Joy couldn't wait to inform Jettie about Vince's loss. She didn't want the conversation to drift into a lot of questioning. She had to warn the girls so they could tell their guys. They needed to be delicate and not put Vince in a difficult situation.

The girls excused themselves to the powder room. The door had barely closed when Joy grabbed Jettie and Dixie. She filled them in on the tragedy.

Dixie had to wipe her tears; she was unable to contain her emotions at the news of Vince's loss. "That is so sad."

After refreshing their makeup and dabbing on lipstick, they returned to the table. The mood was elevated as the night progressed. There was just something unexplainable about being with a lot of people who grew up together. Appearances had changed; some who used to be the most handsome were no longer. Others considered squares or corny had turned out to be dynamic executives. The prettiest were no longer pretty, and the shy little wallflowers had bloomed into the most exotic creatures. Such was the case of Camilla Rosella Fenitti, as was evident when she and Rocco— everyone knew him by Rocky—entered the ballroom. They were a magnificent couple; an aura of celebrity enveloped them. They were not recognizable as the two Italian exchange students who had attended classes at Central High. They had not attended any of the prior reunions, and whatever they had been doing, they apparently had been doing it right. After the surprise wore off, they were a great plus to the already rocking reunion.

Dixie, Joy, Jettie and Camilla once again met in the powder room and huddled to chatter. Krystal popped in the door. "Girls, what have I been missing? Whew, Johnny and I have been making good use of the oldies but goodies music. Oh, my." She stopped. "Are you little Camilla? No way is that you," she said as she grabbed Camilla's hand.

Camilla said, "Krystal, I would have known you anywhere." The joke about girls visiting in the ladies room was true this night. The girls filled in Krystal and Camilla on Vince's loss.

Afterwards, Krystal said, "Johnny is probably standing outside this door waiting for me. I'll talk to you girls later." And off she went.

She planned to share the news with him when the music stopped. "This is by far the best reunion ever," Krystal said to Johnny.

The principal took the microphone. "If you don't know me or remember me, I am Wallace Marsh. I want to welcome each and every one of you back here this evening in celebration of your 40th reunion. Many of you have traveled far to be here tonight, and there are many others who have gone the extra mile to attend. As I call your name, please come to the stage and remain standing. And please hold the applause until all names have been called."

As the group crossed the stage, the monitors showed photos of them as students back in school. People said, "Oh, look! There she is!" or "I didn't recognize you!" and "What a night! Hmm mm look how good looking he was!" As the last couple stepped into line, Mr. Wallace congratulated each one, one for traveling the farthest to attend, the ones who had been married the longest, the couple who had changed the least, a student who was now a Senator, and so on down the line. It seemed the applause lasted ten minutes. With that segment of the ceremony over, the dancing began. The music was incredibly inviting; it was the music of their time—the music that helped so many of them fall in love, and for tonight, it was still 1962.

Around midnight, Krystal and Johnny formed a circle in the middle of the dance floor. They had taken dancing instructions years ago and continued to love the art. They formed two lines for the Stroll, a popular dance back in the day. Everyone strolled down the line between the boys and girls' lines. It was a lot of great fun for all. At this time of the night, two-thirds of the crowd was on the floor, with not an intimidated one in the bunch. No holding back.

Vince and Joy walked with joined hands to the dance floor, and when they weren't dancing, they sat close together. They were lost in one another, in a world of their own. Joy smiled dreamily. "I feel like Cinderella, and I don't want it to be over."

"Let's not let it be. We are adults."

"We're all booked at the hotel and will meet in the morning for breakfast."

Vince smiled coyly. "Lucky me, I am booked. This is where I am staying while in town."

Jettie and Toby talked about the night and all the couples. They had a lot of fun watching everyone mingle, and they loved to share their feelings with each other.

Dixie held onto Chet's arm and paraded him around like a show pony. "I'd like to introduce you to my boyfriend, Chet Tyler."

He was a good sport about it; they shook hands all around, and Chet and Dixie moved on to the next group. He was well received; everyone seemed to like him, and the guys accepted him from the get-go. That would be good for everyone, because several times a year the girls planned a get-together that required the boys to attend.

Joy watched as Vince and Chet talked; they seemed to have a lot in common. It was clear they would become buddies, especially if Vince decided to stick around a while. In fact, they were both fascinated with Tahoe, from the beauty of the snowcapped mountains and winter sports to the sparkling panoramic beauty and the view of the lake through the luscious trees in the spring. It was resort atmosphere year round. They conversed a lot, and Vince told about the selling of his horse ranch and property in Kentucky three years earlier, but he didn't mention the reason he sold it. His wounds were still too raw to share.

The girls visited with Camilla during the evening and got all the details about what she and Rocky had been doing for the past forty years. They learned all about their restaurants and how their love affair began. They spoke of how shy she used to be. As the girls stood by the refreshment area filling their cups, Camilla said, "After we graduated and moved back to Italy, we realized how much we missed what had grown to be our home and where we shared so many memories from our high school days. It was strange; we had never been attracted to each other until we were back in Italy. Rocky worked in the restaurant for a couple of years and met people who believed in him and helped him with financing some of his business dreams."

"Did ya'll date?" Dixie asked.

"Not at first, but we talked a lot on the phone, and when I saw him, mostly in his restaurant, we'd reminisce of Texas and Silver Springs, remembering the dances, ballgames, and all the fun we had while living there. We were just captivated by the old memories; it was so much a part of both of us. Our Texas roots were deeper than we ever realized and wound around our hearts."

Joy, helping herself to some chips and dip, said, "So when did you realize the attraction?"

Camilla blushed, fanning her hand at her cheeks. "It just dawned on us at the same time. Before we knew what had happened, we were hopelessly in love, and he proposed. The wedding was planned, we married in Rome, then immediately honeymooned in Texas." They chose Houston as their home base because of the established business Rocky had pursued for wine import, and Houston had a seaport, so it just made sense.

The last song, "Goodnight, Sweetheart, Well, It's Time to Go" began and they grabbed their partners; even Toby and Jettie joined in. This would wrap up a most memorable night, Jettie thought. She glanced around the floor searching for Joy, and then she saw them. How perfect, she thought. Vince was just what her dear friend needed. The woman Jettie saw a couple of weeks ago had disappeared, replaced by the radiant beauty she saw tonight. Joy had flourished. Jettie's heart was happy; she felt she could burst into song. The evening was magical and it truly rekindled the glow that once burned bright for one of the most popular couples of that era—none other than Joy and Vince. To see them together, holding each other so tenderly, it was if the gap of years had never been; it was as if time stood still until this moment. It was the best time Jettie could remember for the old gang in years; she hated for the night to end.

Vince couldn't believe the effect this woman still had on him. It felt so right, as if they belonged together. He felt intoxicated with her innocent femininity and Southern charm that simply made his blood boil. This feeling stirred up some guilt because of the loss of his Cricket and their sons. He had feelings that he should not feel now, or ever, not since Cricket was no longer a part of the present. Three years since that tragic car wreck that took her and their boys' lives. It wasn't fair, he thought. It was wrong of him to feel this way about another woman. Yet, here he was holding his first love like he had forty years ago. He was torn between his guilt and wanting to hang onto this glorious feeling of being alive, feeling like a man again.

At one time, they'd been so young, so in love; they promised to be together forever. Her rearing and innocence hadn't allowed her to give in to their desires. Vince was driven by the lust of a healthy eighteen-year-old boy in love. He and Joy had loved and petted to the point he was just about insane. She was the best thing that had ever happened to him, such a good girl, trying to live by the standards her parents had taught her. They'd gone steady for two years, and he was at his limit—being with her, smelling her, feeling her body against his. He was at the breaking point. Something had to happen, and it did. He gave in to temptation with a girl who had been teasing and flirting with him all semester. She'd been trying to lure him into cheating on Joy, and one day it happened. He snapped, and it was too late. He had sex with her on several occasions; the rumors circulated throughout the school.

Before long it got back to Joy, who confronted him. He was trapped, so he confessed. It was bad enough, but he wasn't going to continue to lie and deceive her. Vince felt so guilty, trying to explain. It didn't sound right. He loved her, but he needed satisfied. He'd cheated only to satisfy his animal desire, nothing more. He didn't want it to be over with Joy; he never intended to lose her, but he had to let her go, to sacrifice the promises and plans they'd made for their future. He threw it all away. He broke up with her in the latter part of their senior year. He just couldn't stand for his Joy to be the victim of a group of gossiping girls.

Ironically, it was only two weeks before Valentine's Day, sweetheart day, and a few months until the prom. Their plans were cancelled; he ended up not attending. Joy went with some of her friends who had no date plans. It was a special time in her young life, and he had let this happen to her. He was mad and ashamed of himself. He single-handedly destroyed their special love, tarnished it. He had never meant for any of it to happen. It was an understatement to say Joy's disappointment stabbed at him, seeing her bear the humiliation. He didn't know how she managed to keep her head up. But that's the way she was, dainty and fragile, yet when challenged, she gathered strength, overcame and conquered. In his heart, he felt she would never forgive him.

Yet tonight, holding that familiar tiny frame close, they danced. The special feeling was still there. He saw it in her eyes and felt it in her touch. Yes, it was clearly there. He sensed there was more for them, but only time, precious time, would tell. They'd both been through the war in the last few years. She'd barely hit the highlights of the reason her marriage failed and Frank having other children. It didn't make sense to him, but she would tell him when she felt comfortable. He wouldn't push for more. She never seemed to want or need to discuss it. "That's what I pay the shrink for," she said.

Chapter 7

After the reunion, Joy and Vince became the "couple" again at laser speed. They were seen around town at dinner or other social functions. Joy enjoyed sharing all the growth and changes the city had made since Vince left many years ago. After he graduated, he followed through with his folks' plan for him to attend the University of Kentucky, and that was where he met Cricket in his sophomore year. Her background was very similar to his—ranching parents, raised in the horse business. And she was seeking the same degree in Business and Ranch Management, so needless to say, they had a lot in common.

Vince's parents, John and Josie Chandler, were an amazing couple. Josie was as much a horsewoman as John was a true cowboy. Josie rode the horses and helped the hands out on the ranch before she gave birth to Vince, their only child. They vowed that once their family was started, Josie would be a full-time mom and let the men tend the ranch.

Josie adored Vince and catered to his every whim. He was a product of their love, and they would see to it that he would have it all. When he was a toddler, Josie had him on horseback with her. She proudly boasted, "I believe he rode the stallion before he could even walk." She and John loved passionately and were loving parents. They were not able to have another child and lavished all they had on Vince. It was understood his entire life that he would attend college in Kentucky. That was his parents' dream. John saved money during the rearing years and hand-picked the college. Vince followed their plan and enrolled in Kentucky.

The Chandler's sold their ranch in Texas and followed Vince to Kentucky, where they lived out the rest of their lives. They would live to see their dreams complete after Vince and Cricket married, bought their ranch, and planned their family. Cricket gave Vince two sons, twins, Mickey and Monty. John Chandler couldn't have been happier. You would have thought those twins were his, not just grandsons. John's legacy had been fulfilled. He and Josie lived to see the boys grow into fine young men, duplicates of the Chandler men. John saw them turn into young, healthy, good-looking cowboys riding their horses. They helped with training and were a proud asset to their father.

John and Josie passed away before the boys graduated. Vince was glad they didn't have to endure the pain of losing the boys, along with his Cricket. The freak car wreck fifty miles from their home had killed all three. Vince thought if his parents were alive, the accident might have killed them as well. Cricket and the boys were on their way to pick up Champ, a magnificent stallion. He was a surprise for Vince, who had admired him when he and Cricket attended a horse event months before. Cricket bought Champ and made arrangements to bring him home. Vince had no idea his family was on a mission to surprise him on his birthday. Cricket was driving the truck and pulling the horse trailer when it started raining. A car was coming toward them around a curve. It swerved on the slick road, spun out, and they crashed head on. All three of the Chandlers were pronounced dead at the scene.

Vince nearly lost his mind. He barely managed to survive day by painful day. It became obvious that he should sell the ranch. The memories were bittersweet, bringing tears and joy followed by hot salty tears. It ripped his heart out. Cricket's presence was everywhere, from the sunsets they shared, to the clear Kentucky skies full of stars they counted at night from their private veranda as they lay in each others' arms. The memories permeated his soul. Vince could not sustain his loss and remain at their ranch, walking the earth where they first broke ground to lay the foundation of their home. They chose stucco siding and a red tile roof. It was a stately spread in the valley amidst mountains in every direction. The spirited thoroughbreds had run over the pastures, feeling their freedom as the family watched proudly. It tore him apart to walk away and turn his back on so many years of joy, but he had to. He packed his truck with his personal belongings and left their dreams behind. He vowed to never own another horse. That life was history, buried with his loved ones.

Heart to Heart ♥ Forever

After selling out, Vince drove as fast as he could; he tried to outrun his broken heart. His family rested; all five in the family estate. He would go in search of his sanity and maybe, one day, a place to start over. He traveled the U.S. and saw beauty he'd never seen before, ending up in Northern California where he skied the Sierra Nevada's.

It was odd to hold the notice of the reunion while he stood in the post office. For the first time he wanted to attend. His curiosity about the old crowd grew as he pondered what had happened to them.

Now, here he sat, in the old theatre in his home town in Texas with his high school sweetheart, like he had never left and the last forty years were a fairy tale.

He glanced at Joy, still so beautiful with her dark looks and dainty feminine features. Engrossed in the movie, she didn't notice him staring at her. This couldn't be real; he would soon wake up. He was at peace, a feeling he thought he'd never embrace again. Joy was different from Cricket in every way. Cricket had been blond, blue-eyed, petite and feisty. She loved the horses and had been a champion barrel rider. She could ride with the best of them. She was nearly as good as his mama.

He was a million miles away in thought when Joy asked, "Are you all right?"

He smiled. "Yes."

She turned to watch the movie. He felt the urge to reach over and wrap his large hand around her small one. Her soft hand yielded to his wide palm. It was heaven to be in her presence once again. Joy was all woman, and she made him feel all man. She was irresistible, bringing out in him the desire to be her knight, her protector. He wanted to wrap her in his arms and place her high on a pedestal where she would be safe and never get hurt again.

After the movie, Joy took Vince to her private spot in the park, telling him she went there to get away, to regenerate. It was a large park with walking trails and a rather large pond. They had lots to talk about, even after the reunion. Some of their friends from school with nicknames like Peachy, Fudgo, Peanut and Cookie had come to reunions over the years, but had failed to return this year.

"Do you remember Johnny?" Joy asked. "He looked like a movie star and was voted most handsome?"

"Yes, he was Sophomore, Junior and Senior Favorite. Whatever happened to him?"

"Oh, Carol Henning told me that he was a policeman in Anchorage, Alaska and got gun downed while on duty. A prisoner shot him."

"That's terrible. When did that happen? Who did he marry? Did he have any kids?"

"He was thirty-two, and we didn't know the girl he married. And they didn't have children. We heard his wife ordered cremation before his brother arrived from Texas. The family was bitter and never forgave her for it. Rumor has it that his father never recovered."

After the words were out of her mouth, she wished she could take it back. She didn't want to be insensitive, and it had just slipped out. "Oh, Vince, I'm sorry I said that."

"Joy, it's something that was horrible but a part of life. I'm okay."

Talking about the old days made it seem only a few years had passed, not forty.

Vince had been in love with Joy and she with him. Now it looked like they were going to have another chance at love.

Her life had been off track, hopeless, until he reappeared. Now he was a sensual man with a level of maturity he'd not had when they were teenagers. She yearned to touch him; her arms ached to hold him; she felt addicted to him. Joy had never been so drawn to and aroused by any man as she was by Vince. To think that only a few weeks ago she thought she would never tolerate another man in her life.

She had been dying, drowning from life's hard times, then Vince reappeared. It was as if the life waters had rushed over her and she was instantly rejuvenated with luminous life. She said, "I want to enjoy one day at a time."

He reached out and drew her close. Their lips hungrily sought each other; the kiss was romantic, tender and sweet. He wanted to devour her with kisses, bury his head in her bosom and enflame her with the desire that soared through his veins. Was it love? The thought hammered him. Were they caught up in the sentimental fact their love was the first so many years ago, or that his desire for her had never been satisfied? But on the other hand, he didn't want her to think he wanted one thing and had no control of his actions as when he was a teenager. Not a word uttered, he held her. They snuggled. He enjoyed the lingering tingle of his lips where hers had pressed just seconds ago. The minutes wiled away, neither wanting to separate; they wanted the moment to stand still, frozen in time.

"I want to be with you, Joy," he whispered, "never let you go. My heart and arms yearn for you. I can never lose you again. I love you so . . ."

It was music to her ears.

Chapter 8

Chet told Dixie he wanted to visit the McNamaras. "Jettie guaranteed the best T-bone I've ever eaten, and I want to make her prove it."

Smiling, Dixie made the call; she knew what Jettie was capable of. They decided on Sunday. "Jettie," Dixie said, "Chet says his mouth is watering, and he wants his cooked medium."

"Well, girl, you tell him he's in for a big surprise when he finds out it's better than I said it would be!"

Jettie and Toby entertained at their country place. Rarely did they have guests in town at Shangri-Li, their private home. The country place was only five miles out. It was situated back off the road, the long driveway lined with large pecan trees and surrounded by lush pasture. Jettie organized a group to pick pecans in the fall for their holiday baking and her famous pecan pies.

A large stocked tank filled with corn-fed catfish was the favorite place to fish on the property and pull in a nice catch for a Sunday fish fry. It had a long wooden pier that would allow four to fish at the same time. Toby took a few guys to the tank, and the girls did the cooking. Jettie told everyone, "I'll be glad to cook, but someone else will clean the fish." And that is exactly what happened.

The country home featured a wrap-around porch complete with an array of swings and chaise lounges. It was a charmer, homey and warm. When she had large groups of people, Jettie would ring the bell to summons the guests to the dinner table.

After Chet arrived, Toby drove him in the 4-wheeler to explore the pasture. Toby wanted to show Chet where they fished. Toby loved the wide open spaces and enjoyed gazing out at his land. He pointed out to Chet the different neighbors down the road and told him how long they had been there. He and Jettie owned fifty head of cattle, and there were times when they enjoyed attending the auctions. Toby had a total of three ranch hands, the foreman and a couple of cowboys who lived on and maintained their property. Taking care of the herd, horses and other farm animals was a part of the hands' jobs.

Toby drove back to the bunkhouse where the three men shared quarters. The house was built like a tri-plex log cabin with a big kitchen that centered the floor plan, and the three men each had his own private bedroom and bath in opposite areas of the house. It offered a front porch for sitting and whittling at night after supper. There was a ten-stall barn within walking distance from the bunkhouse.

"Chet, these are real cowboys," Toby said and laughed. "All they do is take care of my farm animals, tend the property, mend fences and run the cattle to and from auctions."

Chet was fascinated. "So, how long have they been with you?"

"Oh, I've known them much longer than they've been here. But they have been here for five years. They do whatever I need done, any maintenance on the main house." Toby leaned back. "I don't know if you know, but this is the exact place me and my brothers and sisters were born and raised."

Chet turned to eyeball Toby. "I had no idea. Nobody ever said anything."

"My daddy was a rancher. He had a dairy later in his life, but we always raised cows and we milked by hand."

Chet was caught up in the story.

Toby drove to a location on a hill and stopped between groves of trees. "This is where the old home place stood. I was one of three boys and two sisters. We were country kids that ran barefoot, rode horses bareback, and fished. A lot of the time Mama would clean and cook our catch for supper."

"That must've been the life, buddy," Chet said. "Myself, I was a city kid."

"Me and my brothers milked every day. Mama taught the girls to cook; we always had a large Sunday lunch."

"How is it that you ended up with the land? What about your brothers and sisters?"

"It rather surprised me and all the kids, but Daddy said they had no interest, and I did, so he willed it to me. That was about eight years ago. Then me and Jettie built this home out here five years ago."

Chet enjoyed his time with Toby; he admired him. Toby was a rugged sort, a man's man, yet totally captivated and in love with his Jettie.

"We better head back; Jettie will have those steaks cooked to perfection about now."

"I can't wait to taste them. From what all I've heard, I'm in for a real treat!"

"Yeah, it's not like the kind you get at these truck stops. She only cooks good quality Angus beef."

Lord, when they got within a quarter of a mile from the house, the smell of charcoaled steaks wafted through the air. They followed their noses to a big platter with four thick t-bone steaks, twice-baked potatoes, fresh garden corn, and baked beans that Jettie had just set on the table. She'd made a mean peanut butter pecan pie that cooled in the kitchen window to be served later with home-made vanilla ice cream.

The guys washed up while Dixie May finished setting the tea and hot rolls on the table. For Chet, it was everything the women had promised and more. Later, lounging on the porch and letting their dinner settle, the ranch hands dropped by to say hello. They'd been in town to see a Western movie and eat Mexican food, and were headed back in for the night. Max, Rowdy and Boots were real cowboys like you would see in the arena. They had plenty of experience on the rodeo circuit before they retired from riding bulls.

Saying goodnight, Rowdy tipped his hat to the ladies and said, "We have a big day tomorrow, ladies; we're taking fifteen head to the auction."

Toby piped up, "If you see any young calves, check them out and buy two or three."

They agreed, then piled back in the truck and headed back toward the groves.

Chet and Dixie May thanked Toby and Jettie for the memorable steaks and said goodnight. All the way to Chapel Valley Chet moaned and groaned and rubbed his belly, stating, "That was the best steak I ever had!"

Chapter 9

"Toby and I wouldn't miss it. I'll be in touch and personally guarantee all the gang members will be present and accounted for," Jettie said before she told Camilla goodbye, then cradled the phone.

Camilla and Rocky knew many politicians, celebrities and news people. During their years in business, their sphere of influence had expanded immensely. They were all invited to celebrate the family's new venues. Their restaurant was an elegant establishment, perfect for such events. Eight members of the old gang were invited. A half dozen of the finest imported wines would be uncorked for the first time and introduced that evening. Every dinner served at Fenitti's was served with a tasting of a wine. That strategy perked sales. The wine sales soared that evening.

The festivities included a fine array of Italian cuisine. The number one wine on the list was their vineyard's finest, "Le Camilla Rosea."

The band was a legend in the area and created the perfect environment to dance.

Jettie followed through. They would all ride in Toby's motor coach. He would chauffeur. Toby's little coach was a forty-five-foot Prevost—the Rolls Royce of recreational vehicles. It had everything you could possibly dream of. Riding in it was like riding down a smooth road in your living room. It was plush with a countertop stove, double door fridge with ice and water in the door, washer and dryer, CD, DVD, television, surround sound, fiber optic lighting, and black granite floors. It was the kind of motor home that people stared at, pointed at, or wondered if rock stars owned.

The girls loved an occasion to dress up, visit with each other, and have this wonderful event to attend, chauffeured in luxury. The men made plans to leave at nine a.m., to arrive in Houston about one p.m. Then they reasoned they would have time on their hands, and they might as well score a hit with the ladies. So they conjured up a tour of Galveston, allowing the ladies time to shop the boardwalk. Toby knew of some fabulous seafood restaurants, and he had to take the gang there, where they enjoyed soft shell crab, jumbo shrimp and fried catfish and oysters. "You have to wash it down with a frosted mug of beer," Toby told the guys.

It took them an hour to drive to the coast, drive back, then dress for the evening. The timing was perfect. The boys had done a good job planning.

Fenitti's restaurant parking lot was large, allowing Toby the room it took to drive to the rear of the lot behind the restaurant. He had plenty of space to do a complete turn, maneuver the forty-five-foot coach and pull under a lush shaded area. Houston had lots of large old trees, and the lot resembled a park. Once situated, the guys hopped out, let the huge awning down and pulled the bay area open that housed the television and refrigerator. It was right up their alley. The men placed their folding chairs under the awning, but only a few feet away from the side of the coach, just an arm's length away from the fridge to reach another beer.

"Now this is the life," Johnny said.

"You bet," Toby answered as he popped the tops and passed the beers around, then took a seat to enjoy the time with his buddies. They sipped the cold brew while watching the tail end of a basketball game. Kicked back, they waited for the girls to give up the coach so they could go inside to dress. The men genuinely enjoyed one another's company—the conversation never lagged.

"Man, this has been a superb idea," Vince said, "and I vote we do it several times a year. I'll help buy gas for this guzzler."

"You're in," Toby said.

Then the questions started: "How much gas does this hold and how much to fill it?" When Toby answered, "Six miles to the gallon," they thought Johnny was going to have to call 9-1-1. He was horrified, being a conservative man. "Good grief," he gulped.

They agreed traveling in the motor home was a must-do again and not comparable to a car trip. "It's like sitting in your living room and arriving at your destination totally rested—that is, except for the driver." Vince laughed.

Toby came back with, "Oh, no. This baby is a dream to drive. I have no complaints."

The girls piled out of the home and were greeted with, "Hubba hubba," and "Sweet mama," and a few other chick remarks.

Jettie curtly said, "Flattery won't get you anywhere, boys, but a big old diamond might work!"

The ladies took the men's chairs, and the guys hustled inside to put their duds on while the girls caught their breath. The soft gentle breeze was ushered in as the evening shadows fell.

The leaves rustled and sticks cracked. "Don't let us scare you; it's me and Rocky," Camilla announced. They had come to greet the group and see how the parking accommodations worked out. When they appeared in the light of the television, Camilla said, "Oh good, you girls are already dressed, so it won't be long?"

Jettie stood, wiping off a few leaves caught at her hem, and answered, "We're coming in as soon as the boys finish dressing."

Camilla gave instructions to their table once they entered the building. She had selected one in the midst of the action and close to the dance floor.

Camilla swayed a little, made a motion as if she were dancing, and said, "Ladies, I hope you are wearing your dancing shoes. I promise you will be asked to dance. We cater to a lot of friendly Houstonians, so, men, don't be getting jealous—it's all in good fun."

"Good grief, Camilla," Jettie exclaimed, "I'm too rusty to dance."

"What? Now, Jettie, you were always an excellent dancer."

"I've been married to a non-dancer for thirty-six years. You get rusty!"

"A few spins around the floor and you'll be in the groove. It's just like riding a bike—you never forget!"

"Okay," Jettie said, "I agree to dance with the guys if they ask. But don't be offended, ladies, when Toby doesn't ask you to dance. I have never been able to make the man do it—well, on some rare occasion, possibly!"

At that time the guys piled out of the coach, which started all the women whistling and making remarks. Rocky stuck out his hand and greeted each guy. Toby spouted off with, "You girls sure did smell up the place with all that passion-powered perfume. Did you marinate in it?"

"Now I guess he has transformed himself into Jerry Seinfeld," Jettie popped back.

Laughing, Camilla and Rocky excused themselves and headed back inside to work the crowd.

They secured the coach and left the entrance lights on for later. The couples linked arms and began their walk to the party. Upon rounding the corner, they saw the cars were stacking up; the valets ran to park and make their way back to the next one in line. Toby was impressed by what he saw. He thought it very unusual for a crowd this size to be frequenting a restaurant. He soon found out this was not any old restaurant—a far cry from it.

Jettie smiled, happy with her decision to wear the three-piece silk pant ensemble with the flowing mid-calf tunic split up both sides that flattered her more-to-love figure. The moment she stepped inside the fabulous foyer, she felt she had walked into Little Italy. It was the most magnificent tribute to old Italy she'd ever encountered. Architecture was her passion. The rich foyer oozed good taste. She found herself wondering if it was Camilla's handiwork or if she'd hired a decorator. The floors were twelve-inch diamond cut black granite tiles, centered with two-inch brass inserts. The walls were hand painted murals of the Italian countryside where Camilla and Rocky played as children. One scene actually depicted them as two small children at play. The artist had captured their look and created a masterpiece with the ingenious strokes of his brush. The large portraits were mounted in heavy, tarnished Italian frames. Jettie pondered why they would choose to leave such a lovely old country.

The smell of freshly baked Italian bread filled the air, and a wine bar was operating in the center of the large dining area. Jettie made note of the intimate rooms separated from the main dining facility for couples or small groups desiring more privacy. It was an exquisite restaurant. Much time had been spent on its embellishment, and the owners had captured an ambience that was a rare find.

The restaurant was introducing six new bottles of the Fenitti's line of imported Italian wine, and there were six bottles on each of the reserved tables. There were eight settings at a table. Jettie's table included Toby, Joy, Vince, Dixie, Chet, Krystal and Johnny.

Camilla and Rocky hosted the main table with the invited dignitaries. Simple observation expressed how very sharp Camilla was in business, and Rocky was suave and debonair. They charmed the crowd and made each and every person feel he was the only guest there. A talented couple, Jettie observed.

Jettie and Joy stayed close together as they looked at everything and talked about it all in whispers. Joy said, "Camilla is stunning, but can you believe that Rocky has turned into an Italian stallion? I mean, mercy."

"Life has been sweet to them, my friend."

It was exactly as the girls had predicted; the night unfolded like an oriental fan. It was exhilarating; no one wanted to take a take a potty break with all the activity on the dance floor.

Krystal and Johnny were in their element doing what they did best. They graced the floor with fancy whirls and dips and all the gracefulness of a couple of swans. She fit in his arms perfectly, and they were as one on the floor. The crowd gathered, intrigued by their talent, and applauded and begged for more. The couple didn't seem to mind; they enjoyed being the center of attention, especially while doing one of their favorite things. There was not a bashful one in the group.

Joy and Vince weren't strangers to dancing, either.

Nor were Dixie and Chet, who made such a cute couple. Her petite frame and that luscious head of hair made her stand out in the crowd; she was a looker by all means. Then there was the boyish blond, handsome Vince with his princess Joy.

The guys invited Jettie to dance, and she accepted; it was just as Camilla said. "It comes right back to you." Jettie danced and was having an absolute ball. She was so thankful Camilla invited and she had accepted for this wonderful group of friends—there was nothing like dancing. Jettie smiled to herself. If you've got it, you've just got it!

In between dances and working the crowd, Camilla stopped by their table. "So what do you think, and how is it going?"

Joy and Vince were the only ones at the table. "What's not to like, girl? You and Rocky have outdone yourselves," Joy answered. "And thanks for inviting us."

The guys had scheduled them to leave for home at midnight, which would put them home around four a.m. It would be late, but they could sleep late the next morning.

Jettie returned to the table. She didn't mention it to her friends, but a few times during the evening she felt as if she were being watched. She noticed an attractive gentleman with a beautiful full head of hair with white edging over his ears. He had a glowing tan. She thought he was looking at someone he knew, so she didn't get too excited, but then she caught him staring a second time with a look of interested curiosity. She knew he was going to stop at her chair; she could just feel it. She began to feel panicky. Her hands began to perspire; she looked for Joy, but she was not there. She didn't know how to act, and that was really something for Jettie, who never met a stranger. She turned her head and looked in another direction; she didn't want him to think she was flirting. Everyone was on the dance floor and Toby had disappeared—probably to the men's room. The stranger smiled and stood over her chair. He was even more handsome up close. She was impressed with his perfect teeth that seemed to dazzle.

"I've noticed you're quite a dancer," he said.

A little embarrassed, she blushed, then smiled; she was about to make an excuse, but opted against it. "Well, thanks for the compliment."

He continued, "I would be honored if you would dance with me." Flattered, her first or maybe second impulse was to accept, but she turned to see if Toby would mind. He was still gone. She extended her hand to the stranger. He guided her to the floor and took her in his arms. Any negative thoughts vanished; she savored the feeling of being admired, to be chosen out of a crowd of attractive women. She let herself go. They circled and floated around the floor. She could feel eyes upon her. Jettie decided she was not going to be robbed of the sublime pleasure and waste time with worry. It was divine; she felt beyond desirable. She enjoyed every twirl. When they'd finished, he escorted her back to the table, leaned over, pressed his soft lips to the back of her hand, and said, "Madame, it has been my ultimate pleasure."

If she weren't so happily married, this man could rock her world. She grabbed a wine menu lying close by and began to fan at her chest. She had gotten excited after this little whirl around the floor and felt somewhat giddy, like a young girl at her first dance. She had to get her composure back and settle her jets. Jettie looked around for her soul mate, but he was nowhere to be seen. She shrugged and then shared the story with one of the girls. No telling how long that flattery would last her; she still felt light headed from the experience.

No one had seen Toby. He'd made his way back from the men's room and caught a glimpse of his Jettie being whirled around the dance floor like a professional dancer. Bowled over, he stood in the shadows, then ripped apart the artificial foliage, just like in the movies, and watched his woman in the arms of a mysterious stranger. He only knew one thing–the green-eyed monster was alive and well. He used to feel it when other men admired Jettie or while others openly flirted with her. She never gave him anything to be jealous about anymore. As a young woman, she knew how to pull his strings, and did so when she felt it necessary to jerk his chain to get him in line, as she used to tell Joy.

Jettie had gotten settled from the dance by the time some of the girls asked who the stranger was.

"Leave it to Jettie to draw one like a magnet; we can't leave you alone for five minutes," Joy said. "And where is Toby?"

Jettie answered, "Now, you know he's probably in the men's room."

Toby arrived on cue, pulled out his chair, and scooted closer to Jettie.

The conversation was quickly redirected as Krystal began asking Toby questions about the coach, moving the conversation right along. Ten minutes passed, then a dreamy ballad began to play. Toby leaned over and whispered in Jettie's ear, "Hey, sexy, they're playing our song."

She was more than a little surprised, yet pleased. She followed him to the dance floor and he swept her away. Toby could dance as well as the next, if he were in the mood. And, for some reason, he seemed to be in the mood. Her lips turned up and she teared a little; she knew that Toby must have seen the handsome stranger dance with his Jettie, and that started his motor running. She was pleased; she cuddled closer and laid her head on his chest. He softly kissed her forehead and held her familiar body as he hummed to the tune. She knew how fortunate she was to be loved by this man. In the circle of these protective arms, close to forty years after they'd first begun, he still made her heart happy. She closed her eyes and savored this moment; their hearts beat as one. He dipped and swayed her; she never missed a queue. No man would ever take his place.

Another chapter came to an end for these friends of four decades. They approached the coach after saying goodbye. They were all talked out and ready to relax. Jettie suggested to all it would be a good idea to change into comfy travel clothes; the drive would take four hours to their cars. Toby, the captain of his ship, took his place behind the big wheel; he was in his element. He adjusted the interior lights to off, leaving a hint of soft accent lights aglow. Their friends scattered to their designated places, some lay; others sat. Jettie fluffed her pillow and passed around small travel throws. When they pulled out of the lot, she said, "You would be wise to get a cover, because Toby will freeze your fanny off. In fact, you might wonder where he hangs the meat."

When Toby drove, he had a habit of tuning in his favorite '50s station; it helped him stay awake, but mainly he loved the music, and so did Jettie. Oh, what a night, a perfect ending for a perfect night. The doo-wop sound of their generation floated through the speakers in rich tones as the romantic lyrics of "Earth Angel" filled the plush bus. The lucky riders were on their fantasy trip back home by way of cloud nine.

Chapter 10

A lot of things had happened since that party in Houston. It was the time of year when the seasons began to change. The winds picked up, and the crisp night air required a light wrap. The girls were all communicating by telephone, and a few of them emailed regularly. It was the holiday season, which placed high demand on all their time, most being business owners.

They abandoned the idea of a retreat and decided to wait until later, possibly February, taking all the schedules into consideration.

The meeting place was unanimously chosen to be at Jettie's, the hostess queen. She would lay out the red carpet, and it would be a new time to remember. They were used to going there and hanging loose. Her home just had a relaxed resort atmosphere, and it was hard to leave after you'd been there a while. Their plan was to cook steaks and lounge out on the porch that wrapped entirely around the white two-story house with black shutters adorning each window.

Jettie kept all types of lounge chairs and lap wraps. She provided her guests the best of the good life and never missed a detail. Even though it would be February, in Texas, you just rolled with the flow. It could freeze one day and soar to the eighties the next. The Texas sun in February could work out just fine; they would just play it by ear.

Plans were made to load up and investigate some of the well-known antique shops in the area. A 1950-60s classic car show and parade was scheduled for that weekend—the hot cars of their youth. The days when they cruised and ruled the streets of Silver Springs. That promised to be a lot of fun, and then they would vote for the best car in the show. That night they went to the local drive-in and stuffed themselves on cheeseburgers, French fries, onion rings and malts. The scales would not be their friends the next day, Jettie told the girls. When they rallied, it was not the time to diet. The guys had no mercy on Camilla and Jettie as they tried to discuss carbohydrates and calories. Camilla, defeated, said, "Oh well, what's another five pounds; we'll just have to starve next week!"

There was another new item that'd surfaced since they were teens. Joy told Vince, "Believe it or not, you have got to try this!"

He said, "What is it?"

"You won't believe it, but here it comes." She popped it into his mouth before he knew what was happening.

"What is this? Is it a pickle?"

"Absolutely," Joy reported. Dipped in a little ranch dressing, it tantalized the taste buds.

"Well, you know what they say about Texans," Vince said. "They'll fry up anything."

At the end of the fun weekend, all the friends went their separate ways to meet the challenges in their personal worlds. They'd all turned out to be more than the average achiever. This was a group of entrepreneurs who owned their own businesses in many diversified areas, which made them an interesting bunch of people. Even with their busy schedules, the phone lines from south Texas to Central to East Texas were pumped steadily to life as everyone called to check up on and keep up with their dear friends.

After all the sparks too flame between Joy and Vince at the reunion last spring, they had not missed a step with each other. It was reminiscent of the "Sleeping Beauty" fairy tale. Sleeping Beauty slept for so many years, only to awaken when the handsome prince kissed her. Why that was exactly what had happened to Joy.

Instead of simply living to live, they were now living to love, and they only had eyes for each other. What a glorious feeling to have found each other again after a whole lifetime. There were years left, and they wanted to spend them together.

All the heart-to-heart gang expected that Vince and Joy would marry one day—it seemed as they destiny had smiled on this relationship.. Here they were on the brink of starting life over—together.

The buzz was about Dixie and Chet. What started out so sweetly now made them a bit suspicious. It was agreed—the girlfriends thought the relationship had hit a sour note. When the girls were chatting either by email, text message, or phone, they seemed to always be sharing an update on the couple. It wasn't as gossip; these women loved and cared for one another, and frankly, they didn't want to see one another suffer. They were always on duty to watch out for a friend's backside. It was just that simple.

The latest was that Chet had changed. The old cliché—he wasn't as attentive as he once was. The girls were about as tight as a fiddle string, they were no longer a fan of Chet's by any stretch of the imagination. Dixie broke down with her dirty laundry and wrote some messages on email and admitted the problem to her friends. She wrote, "Chet shows his other side behind closed doors. He talks terrible to me in private."

"That's what I've always called a snake in the grass," Jettie said.

Dixie managed to keep it to herself for quite a while, until it had affected her appearance. Her face was haggard and drawn, and her weight was down, her eyes deep set. Her friends saw the change but kept quiet. They decided she was so busy burning up the road with him and working long hard days at the shop that she was probably just exhausted.

Jettie had Chet figured out from the get-go, and the other gals had him pegged in six months. Jettie said, "I have wisdom about people; it's an instinct, just like my Mama had." And there was a lot of truth in those words.

Furthermore, Jettie made remarks to Joy on more than one occasion. "I've noticed the way Star acts with Chet when she thinks no one is looking." Star was a young hottie, older than her years with short black hair, but enough flipped around to make for a very provocative hairdo. She looked as if she had been melted into her Capri's and tight-fitting tops, which were the trend of the time. She wore tons of bangles and beads. She was a hot mama.

Dixie told her girlfriends one day when they were walking in the park, "I don't care what she does about flirting with the men, it doesn't hurt my male trade, and she pulls it together when there are ladies in the shop."

Toby told Jettie one day while they talked on the cell phone, "Hey, that looks like Chet riding with Star in her car."

"Where are they?" Jettie asked.

"She's headed out on Old 19."

Jettie clutched the phone tighter. "You need to tell Dixie May."

"No way. I'm not even sure it's him. And don't you ever say anything about it to her. It would just start something."

Later, Dixie May confessed, "I'm still a sucker; I thought it was true love." She cried and blew continuously. His disrespect for her turned into physical abuse. In the beginning, Chet had put a hard luck story on Dixie; he got to her for some of her savings toward a real estate investment and even talked Dixie into using her car as a down payment for a new truck for him. That left her with a gas guzzling truck and a big fat payment to go with it, which he promised to pay.

Jettie wondered how Dixie could have been such a chump with this Romeo. "So what happened to his big shot job? Didn't that pay a big salary?" Jettie asked.

Dixie answered, "His ex-wife said he owed thousands in back child support and alimony too, and she threatened to put him in jail if he didn't cough up the money."

"How do these types of men get inside a woman's head?" Joy asked.

Dixie May offered, "First they get inside your heart." She ducked her head, heartbroken and shamed—a look these friends never wanted to see on her face again.

"Let me just say," Dixie said, "I thought we were planning our future together. Now I realize that he played me for a fool. "

"Well, that was when you were thinking with your heart and not your head," Jettie said.

When they lunched with her, she was a sad sack; and she couldn't manage to even be happy for a short time. The funny, perky gal who wore all the high heels and gabbed her way through customer after customer was a mere shadow of her old self.

Several months dragged by, and the friends kept close tabs on Dixie May. She worked, went home, changed into some drab old robe, pulled her blinds, and sat in silence. Her pretty bouncy hair was a mess. She had dark circles under her eyes from not sleeping at night. Many days she came to work with little or no sleep.

The girlfriends were on high alert, at their wits' ends as to what to do. She would not agree to see a doctor. It was unanimous; they reasoned it had to be a nervous breakdown. And it was all because of Chet breaking up with her and leaving town, they thought.

Dixie had no family; she had lost both parents about ten years ago, one right after the other. Her one sister had moved away; they were never close. The closest people she had to family were her heart-to-heart friends.

It was rumored that Chet had been seen back in town a few times. The gossip was he had some loose ends to finish up with his job. Then Jettie heard through a customer that Chet was seeing another woman in town. Seemed he had been seen on the outskirts late at night a couple of times this last month. The first thing Jettie thought of was Toby's remark when he'd thought he saw Chet in Star's car, but he wasn't sure, and made her promise to keep her mouth shut.

Now her gut told her that Toby was right, and it had been Chet. What Jettie didn't understand was why he would be sneaking back into town. It didn't make any sense.

Joy felt terrible and helpless about Dixie, and even guilty because she and Vince were so in love and making plans to wed. The date was only six months away. Jettie was helping to organize plans for the wedding. Joy and Vince were to marry on the boat that hosted wedding parties in Lake Tahoe. That's where Vince told Joy he wanted to marry her, and she accepted.

Jettie and Toby couldn't be gone but a quick two days at that time of year. It was buying season for the store. Toby shared their friend's plans to marry in Tahoe and the fact that he and Jettie could not be gone but a couple of days to Ben, a personal friend of his. Then something happened that Toby never dreamed of. Ben offered to fly the couple to the wedding and fly them back in his private Cessna airplane. Toby talked with Jettie, and they accepted the invitation.

Jettie was an idea person, and she dreamed up a doozy for the wedding. She and Toby conjured up an idea to make a banner that could be flown behind the small aircraft. It would read "Heart-to-heart ~ forever." The plan was for them to circle the hotel when everyone was standing on the terrace waving their goodbyes. The banner would automatically be turned loose to fly directly behind the plane.

Toby said, "This is the ultimate surprise for the newlyweds, and a special message to Joy from the sisterhood."

Being pleased with their cleverness, they giggled and jumped around, hugging each other. The owner of the plane, Ben, was to keep the banner stored until the perfect time for releasing it.

Chapter 11

The only dark cloud on the horizon was the one lingering over Dixie.

All the friends except Dixie had made plans to attend the happy occasion. Her shop was suffering; customers left and had taken their business to other local shops. Trudy and Star were still with her, but it was as if Dixie had lost her will to live.

Joy told Jettie one day, "If she keeps this up she won't have enough customers to pay the rent."

The land developer who owned her building had doubled her rent, saying that everyone else it town had done the same. He owned lots of other small strips, and he'd been more visible than ever in the last six months. That is, ever since he opened his office across the parking lot. But, apparently he couldn't see past the dollar signs and hadn't noticed that her increase in business this year had dropped off significantly in the last couple of months.

"Oh, well. He didn't have a classy reputation; he was known for his greed. Word was he didn't care about the people—just show him the money," Trudy fussed.

Joy and Jettie had stopped by to check on Dixie, and Trudy had time to talk. Dixie hadn't arrived at the shop yet, opposite of the way she used to be. Trudy went on to say that Pete, the landlord, gave her the willies, since he was always dropping by for one thing or another. "I don't know, there's just something strange about him."

"Well, do you mean like a pervert or something?" Joy asked

"No," Trudy said, "he just has a way of staring. I don't know."

"Isn't he married to a nice woman who volunteers at the Community Hospital?" Joy asked. "I don't know her name. I think they've been married a long time, and supposedly they moved here about fifteen years ago."

"What's even stranger," Trudy said, "is that she doesn't get her hair done here. She goes to Wanda's across town, but he's in here every week. Star trims his hair. He says he can't stand it touching his collar." Trudy laughed. "And as cheap as he is, Star don't cut him any slack; she charges more than anybody in town. Oh, and get this," she continued, "last month he started getting his nails manicured and buffed every week. It seems weird to me. I know, because I'm the one who does his nails, and he can hardly sit still for eyeballing Star. I don't keep up with everybody, but this guy is strange."

"Are you afraid to be with him?" Jettie asked

Trudy shook her head. "No, but he doesn't come unless me and Star are both in. He doesn't have any dealings with Dixie May, except collecting the rent. I just don't get it. But, I wish Dixie May would pull herself together."

"Trudy," Jettie said, "let me ask you a question. What do you know about Chet and Dixie's relationship?"

Trudy walked and piddled with different things as she talked, then stopped and placed a hand on her hip. "Well, it's like all of this we're talking about. You see and hear everything in a beauty shop; there isn't any privacy." She asked the girls if they wanted a cold drink from the box.

Joy passed, but Jettie said, "Do you have Diet Pepsi?"

"Diet Coke."

"That's good."

Trudy got it and carried it to Jettie, then went on to finish her story. "For a long time it seemed to be good between Dixie and Chet." She paused as if remembering and sat in a chair. "He began to change in his behavior to Dixie, but she continued to drool and cater to him." Trudy rolled her eyes. "And he got to where he talked downright hateful to her, then that got to be his habit. I wouldn't have another man if they gave me one."

Trudy had been a widow for ten years, and she said waiting on her late Carl nearly killed her. She went to the front desk and straightened it up as she talked.

Jettie and Joy remained sitting in the operator's chairs, and as Trudy moved around the room, they just turned the revolving chairs.

"Did he act or talk ugly to anyone else, customers or you?" Joy asked.

"He treated me okay. I really didn't have much to do with him. I could take him or leave him," Trudy remarked.

Jettie said, "Well let me ask you something else. How did he treat Star? I know other men seem to like her."

"Oh, girl, Chet was nice to Miss Star, more so than anyone. Many times they would ride together to get our lunches, or he'd run to the beauty supply store with her so he could carry the boxes in." Again, she made a face of disbelief. "I think he's a sneaky womanizer, and for some reason he turned on Dixie and treated her like dirt under his feet. I always thought he had too much interest in Star; it was obvious. I could see the women in the shop raise their eyebrows and exchange looks when he was acting cute in front of Star at Dixie's expense."

"Well, what did Dixie do?" Joy asked.

"Oh, she appeared to ignore them. If it bothered her, you couldn't tell it. He was around for about nine months, and he wasn't the way he used to be."

Jettie and Joy said they had to leave and couldn't wait any longer for Dixie May, so they would catch her another time.

Trudy walked them to the door. "Please don't repeat what I've said. I'm just worried about Ms. Dixie. And I hate what is happening to her. I just want to help."

Jettie patted her on the shoulder. "Girl, don't worry about it. We don't intend to tell her anything; we are as concerned as you are. Your words are safe with us." She smiled at Trudy and they left the salon.

When Jettie and Joy reached the car, they were both fuming.

"I had a feeling about that damn Chet and that tight britches ho," Jettie said. "I knew that slime ball and trailer trash were up to something!"

"You never said anything like that."

"Toby thought he saw Chet one day in Star's car, but he wasn't sure. They were headed out of town, and not to the lunch counter or the hair supply! Toby made me promise not to say anything. I had my own feeling about those two. It was just a gut feeling, nothing more. I think what I'm madder about is the way he's treated our dear Dixie May. It makes me mad and sad."

While they both agreed, what in the world could they do about it? They knew one thing for sure, come hell or high water they had to get Dixie somewhere for help, because this could clearly devastate the rest of her life at the rate she was going. "She may never pull out of the slump," Jettie said, "at least not by her own will at this point."

"And furthermore," Joy added, "what do you think about this weirdo landlord hanging around suddenly? When I think about it, it sounds like both of those men are making a point to hang around that Star kid."

"She's only twenty years old, and men are so stupid sometimes and make such fools out of themselves," Jettie grumbled while she fished gum from her purse.

They stopped to pick up Jettie's car, and then went in separate directions. They both had a lot going on and couldn't devote any more time to Dixie's problem. They had their own fires to put out. Jettie had to get home to Toby, and Joy and Vince were expected for dinner at Jules'.

Things were working out to perfection for Joy. It was great to see her so happy again, Jettie thought. It was sad that Vince's wife and twin sons had been killed. Jettie had no idea how he managed to live with that. She had been there when Joy and Frank's marriage ended up in the toilet. She concluded that one never knew what could happen next. But she knew one thing for sure, she couldn't be happier for Joy and Vince. They were getting another chance at life and happiness.

Weeks flew by, and none of the friends had been together lately, only communicating by phone, or cell, and certainly email. Camilla was a stickler for email messages. She and Jettie kept the communication busy with that technology. Krystal and Johnny were flitting in and out of town; they were truly made for each other and found more romantic get-aways than anyone. Krystal had offered to lend Jettie and Toby her candles and matches, saying she never left them at home. You never knew when you might want to stage a romantic setting. It was obvious that Krystal and Johnny loved each other deeply and truly enjoyed their time together. They worked hard at staying in love. Krystal said, "Our love was a spark that caught on fire."

Joy and Vince were busy getting everything set up for the wedding, and had flown to Tahoe on a couple of weekend trips to select the exact materials and decorations. On the last trip, they house hunted, and decided to cruise through an area in Truckee, which was just across the Nevada line in Northern California, in the Sierra Nevada Mountains. It was breathtakingly beautiful, and the town captivated the couple.

A large log home caught their attention during the drive. Stopping in front, they took down a number. Nestled in the tall and abundant trees, the driveway wound its way through the tangled forest to the front of the home. It was positioned to view Lake Tahoe in any season, and the sight was spectacular. They called the number on the sign, and the real estate agent met them at the vacant property.

When they walked through the door, they knew this was to be their future home—it was instant love. The square footage sprawled on one level with a huge stone fireplace in the center of the house. An open kitchen flowed into the living room with a large wrap-around bar. The master bedroom was on one end and two other bedrooms on the opposite end. A deck in the back housed a massive barbeque pit with a hot tub on the end. It was in primo shape and obviously had been loved and cared for by the previous owner. The freshly painted interior was ready for a new owner. The owners had been transferred to Costa Rica unexpectedly. After walking around, checking it out and talking with the agent, they decided to make an offer on the spot. The realtor wrote the offer leaning on the hood of his car. If the owner took it, then they knew it was meant to be. They asked for an answer in no more than two days.

Quite surprised, they got a call the very next day from the agent saying the contract was accepted with no changes, and she had already delivered it to the title company.

Immediately upon arriving at home Joy called Jettie with the thrilling news. Since that time, the women had been busy creating Joy's Truckee home. With the furniture store, everything needed was right at Jettie's fingertips. In just a few weeks, she and Joy selected, purchased, had delivered, completely furnished and decorated the newlyweds-to-be's Truckee home. The gorgeous ranch house nestled amongst the huge trees with the incredible crystal blue lake serving as their landscape was a dream come true.

Joy told Jettie, "Our new house is awaiting me and my honey to cross the threshold and claim it as the home where we will live happily ever after."

The girls got so excited to hear Joy express that, they hugged and squealed with unbelievable delight.

Dixie was still withdrawn and defeated. Many days, the friends called the beauty salon and no one answered. They knew the business must have really been suffering. So far, Dixie had dodged them when they called trying to take her to lunch.

One day, they did stop in and Dixie was there. She looked like a stranger. Her hair had been cut to a much shorter length; she wore very little make-up, and her eyes were literally sunk into her head. Things were not going well. It seemed that Dixie was running low on money and out of time.

Trudy called Jettie one day, and said she thought she was going to be leaving. Her finances were suffering; she wasn't married and had to make her living. She further took the liberty to tell Jettie that Chet had made several phone calls to Star; Trudy knew it was him because she answered the phone. She said that you could tell he was trying to disguise his voice, but she knew it was him. She then said she had been by Dixie's, and she had let her in a few times the last couple of weeks. Trudy stated that the place was a mess and it smelled like the trash had not been taken out. It was obvious that Dixie had lost all sense of reality and pride.

"I think maybe I made a mistake. I told her Chet had called Star. She looked at me but didn't say a word. She just had a blank look on her face. But I wish I could have taken it back. Why did I do that?" Trudy said.

When Joy received a call from Jettie, she immediately called Dr. Avery about Dixie's state of mind and all that had transpired. He told Joy that Dixie needed to be evaluated immediately and probably checked into a mental facility for a short time. He felt they could do great things for her and help her get back to her old self.

Joy called Jettie, and they decided to go to Dixie's unannounced and make her go with them to see Dr. Avery, then let him determine what to do next. It was agreed that Joy would pick up Jettie at nine a.m. sharp the next morning and proceed straight to Dixie's. They said goodnight, feeling satisfied a plan of action was in place to help their dear friend.

That morning, the town of Chapel Valley was buzzing. This was the biggest thing they had ever seen. At all the local coffee shops the early morning regulars were talking about one thing and one thing only. A couple was found shot to death in the motel down in Pecan Bend, about ten miles out of Chapel Valley. When the maid went into a room to clean it about ten a.m., she found them lying in pools of blood on the bed. The coroner's report stated that the shooting appeared to have happened sometime between three and four a.m. The police were immediately notified, and every squad car from Pecan Bend, and a couple from connecting counties, were at the crime scene. So far names had not been released. An inside source leaked that the man checked in about midnight and he was alone. They had no information concerning when the woman arrived; no one saw her until the maid discovered both bodies in the room.

Joy and Jettie were en route to pick up Dixie. Neither of the ladies had bothered to turn on the radio; they were on a mission, and they had their minds focused on Dixie. They had no idea of all the chaos that was going on in Pecan Bend and Chapel Valley. They were dumbfounded to see a squad car sitting in front of Dixie May's house. They sat paralyzed in the seat of the car as they watched two policemen escort Dixie out of her house handcuffed. She looked frightened and in shock. Dixie May saw her girlfriends and shouted to them, "Help me. I have no idea what's going on! Girls, help me! Lord, just help me, please!"

She was sobbing uncontrollably. Jettie and Joy ran to the officers and demanded to know what was going on. All they would say was that she was under arrest, and instructed them to stand back out of the way. An officer guided Dixie May's head as she bent into the back seat of the squad car. Dixie May looked pitiful as the two women stood helplessly by, watching their friend be whisked away.

Jettie and Joy ran back to the car, grabbed their cell phones and immediately started dialing. When Toby answered, Jettie hysterically said, "Toby, Dixie's been arrested, and I have no idea why."

"Jettie, everything's going to be okay. Stay right there; it will take me about forty minutes to reach you, but I don't want you to leave. And Jettie, they've just announced breaking news that a couple has been discovered murdered at that Pecan Bend Motel down by the lake."

"Who were they?"

"They didn't give any details. There will be more information on the murders at noon on channel three."

Jettie, turning to Joy, was about to tell her what Toby had said when she realized Joy was talking to Vince. She got quiet for a few minutes, then poked Joy. "Joy, they found a couple murdered in Pecan Bend at a motel. Toby just saw it on television."

Joy stopped talking abruptly and stared at Jettie. "What did you say?"

Jettie repeated it.

Joy turned to her cell phone. "My God, Vince, please hurry! I'm so frightened. I need to have you close. Please hurry, darling." Then she hung up. "He's on his way," Joy said.

"Toby will be here as soon as he can drive from Silver Springs to Chapel Valley. Where was Vince?"

"He was having breakfast out on the highway between Chapel Valley and Silver Springs. It won't be long."

"Toby told me to sit still until he arrives, but I can't. I have to get up and move around a little." She opened the door and Joy followed suit. They decided to stroll down the block and back to relieve stress.

"Joy, is everything going to be okay? Could this be some kind of misunderstanding?"

Joy simply answered, "I have no idea what to think."

They strolled silently. It didn't seem too long before Toby arrived, and behind him, Vince pulled up. The men were their rocks. Each one hugged his lady and gave her the support she so needed at this time. They stood together, then decided to go to a local coffee shop and let all this emotion settle down before driving back home the forty miles.

"We are in Podunk Squat, Texas. Nobody gets killed in this tiny hole in the road place," Joy said. "The worst thing I ever heard of was someone being arrested for a DUI." She stirred her coffee and shook her head.

Neither woman could ever recall a single murder in their entire lifetime in or around their hometown. "I can hardly breathe," Jettie said. "Maybe I'm hyperventilating."

Toby put his arm over her shoulder. "Now, Jettie, I want you to get yourself under control. This won't do any good, and it certainly won't help Dixie."

"I'm so scared," Joy said.

"Exactly why are you scared?" Jettie asked.

"Because I have a bad feeling that Dixie may have had something to do with those murders."

"Oh, Joy, your imagination is out of control with all of this chaos." Jettie shook her head, but she wondered. She didn't speak it, but could it be true? Could that dead man be Chet, and could Dixie May have done it? She thought it best not to say it and upset Joy even further. They mulled over the past few months, remembering Dixie changing. Her entire demeanor bore no resemblance to the previously pretty, vivacious redhead who now appeared to be a shell of that woman. She had taken on a homeless look; deep set eyes and her once clothing, gay and fun, was dreadful.

Their intent today had been to get her to Dr. Avery's for his evaluation, then adhere to his recommendation and strategy for Dixie May's recovery, and they had no doubt that was feasible. With their minds made up they would take whatever measures necessary to restore their friend to a healthy state of mind.

Jolted by remembrance of their appointment, Joy squealed, "Oh, my Lord, I forgot to call Dr. Avery's office; they're waiting on us." She was able to speak with Dr. Avery, and he advised her to get in touch with Jules. She will need a good attorney.

Vince didn't have much to say upon arrival, other than he just could not believe all this was happening in this cottage community.

Heart to Heart ♥ Forever

Chapter 12

Across town, to say that Illiana Winn's day had started strangely was an understatement. She and her husband, Pete, had been married fifteen years and relocated to Chapel Valley as newlyweds. A friend of Pete's told him there were plenty of depressed real estate opportunities in that area. The market had crashed several years before, and it was time to buy low and resell at a premium. Peter Winn knew how to make that happen more than anyone she had ever had the pleasure to know. It seemed he had the Midas touch, and everything he touched turned to gold. He could make anything happen, except he and his beautiful wife were unable to have children.

Illiana lost three babies in the first five years of their marriage. The doctors advised she would never be able to carry to full term. After much disappointment, they accepted their destiny, deciding to make the most out of their childless lives. Neither could warm to the idea of adoption, especially Pete.

They lived a quiet life and enjoyed many of the privileges that some people only dreamed of. When in New York City, they stayed in the best hotels and took in Broadway shows. They equally enjoyed their season membership at the Myerson Concert Hall in Dallas. Travel was in their blood, and they could afford to go first class to any destination they chose. She purchased tickets at Pete's first whim, and they would spend Christmas in Russia, or see all the sights that Paris has to offer. The world was at their fingertips. Illiana loved Pete, so it was easy to adjust to their losses and fully enjoy the life of luxury.

For years, Pete had been a devoted husband and lover. But lately he seemed to have lost interest. Illiana reasoned it was because of their ages and getting settled in and comfortable with each other. She dealt with that very well. She allowed him space to work and pursue their living, and he did a wonderful job.

They often had Sunday brunch at the local country club, where they were members. Pete golfed for fun, and Illy took tennis lessons and played Mahjong with the club ladies. She didn't need to earn an income, and Peter actually preferred her to be free at a moment's notice. It made her happy to devote her spare time to volunteer work. Illiana had a special place in her heart for the elderly and looked forward to delivering meals on wheels each week. At times she would help at the hospital in the cancer and heart wings, visiting with the families of the patients. Her life was full and happy and she had no complaints.

That was until approximately four months ago. Her man, the one she could literally set her watch by, began to change. He missed meals, arrived home late, or missed appointments with clients. She was most concerned by the abrupt onset of the strange behavior. She would awaken in the middle of the night and his bed would be empty. If she inquired where he was, he'd mumble that one of his rental units had an emergency, nothing more.

They had always slept in the same bed, but he recently complained of backaches and not being able to rest, purchased twin beds. She believed married couples should always sleep in the together. She knew for a fact her father would have it no other way. The disappearing pattern became more frequent.

In the beginning, Illiana believed the emergency stories, but as it became routine, she grew suspicious. He had never before given her reason to distrust him.

Last night was the final straw. She told him goodnight and pretended to take her nightly sleeping pill. She settled into her bed, faking sleep. Illy was going to get to the bottom of this weird habit, one way or another. It was difficult to remain alert when it was still and quiet. Her eyes got heavy, but sheer will kept them open. It worked. About two a.m. she heard his covers rustle. She was impressed—he'd gotten very astute at deceit. Even listening intently, it was hard for her to make out his moves. Occasionally, she would have to peer between the tiny slits of her eyelids. Her plan was to jump into her clothes and get to the car before he left the corner.

Whatever it took, she was going to follow him to whom or what it was that drove him out of her home on those late nights. It worked exactly as planned.

She followed far enough behind so as not to attract attention to herself. Her car was black, which was in her favor. They traveled outside the city limits. All the while she wondered where he could possibly be going. They got to a stretch of country where she had to fall back a quarter of a mile to avoid being conspicuous. Hoping to appear as a late night traveler, she kept her speed consistent.

Finally, they entered the city of Pecan Bend, population 3,299, ten miles south of Chapel Valley. He caught a red light and she decided to pull over to the side of the road and douse her lights. She sat there. When the light changed, he made a right. She started up and proceeded, then turned in the same direction. Illiana could see his taillights as he drove straight ahead toward a neon light that she could almost read—and then it was clear—Pecan Bend Motel. He pulled in and disappeared into the center of the motel. She decided to park then dash over to see what she could at close range. Once seeing the layout of the motel, she thought he'd certainly see her car if she pulled into the square-shaped parking lot.

It was a small, old two-story motel with probably no more than fifty rooms. Illiana squeezed behind a bush and the building and made her way around the corner. It was so quiet her breath sounded like a train. Glancing slowly around the lot, she locked him into her vision. He was parked in a corner as if hiding or to make a quick get-away. She strained to see him better; he was still in his car.

Laughter rang out in the still black night. A playful couple appeared, talking and bumping each other with their hips as they hurried along. They laughed all the way to the ice machine. As the young woman bent over to gather ice, the older man seductively ran his hands over her body. She giggled with delight. She slapped at his hands, which only made him more playful. She grabbed a handful of ice and threw it at her lover. Then they ran back to their room, wildly giggling, and slammed the door.

Pitch-black silence fell over the eerie night, magnified by the absence of the amorous couple. Out of the corner of her eye, Illiana saw movement, and turned to see Pete get out of his car. He walked in the shadows, staying close to the walls.

She had seen quite enough. He was obviously in pursuit of a rendezvous with some woman. It was bad enough she'd stooped to crouching in the bushes of this grungy-looking motel like some night stalker. She was hurt enough. Why wait to see him in the arms of another woman? No! She had to flee.

She felt like a snake in the grass, slithering her way back to her car. Illiana drove with lights out until she reached the main highway back to Chapel Valley. Desperate to be home, she floored the accelerator.

Illy fumed. She went over and over all the details of what she had seen. The very idea that he had an affair in that grungy motel made her want to puke. Needing to suck clean night air into her lungs, she rolled down her window. Her stomach churned; rage followed. Overwhelmed with a feeling of "woe is me" made for a miserable ride back home, one that would not soon be forgotten. She looked at her car clock; it read three-thirty a.m. She groaned and wondered if she'd ever feel the same about her life after tonight. Unlocking the house, she walked directly to the sofa and stretched out full length on her stomach. The old familiar overstuffed pillows let her burrow in their warmth while she released a torrent of tears.

Her thoughts rambled. She was wracked with emotions. Her nose was now stuffed up, and her cheeks and eyes burned with irritation from the salty tears. She tried to think of excuses; after all, it might have been a huge misunderstanding. He could have located a tenant owing him a lot of money and skipping a lease. That would prompt him to action. He wasn't afraid of anything or anybody when it came to his money.

Mulling it over, it really did make sense. But on the other hand, she tried to remain logical. The stories he supplied regarding the emergencies in his buildings were weak, and frankly, just did not ring true. The gut feeling she had was right on target. He was guilty of something; she just didn't know what.

It was about an hour later when she heard the sound of a car rolling onto the gravel of the driveway. The car lights were off. Peeking out, she saw Pete. Illiana quietly made her way back to the sofa to wait for him in the dark. She sat there with her fingers ready to switch on the light the minute he was in the room. She wanted to catch him off guard. Deep down she hoped he had an excuse for this hellish nightmare. Illy strained her ear to hear any noise from outside. Where was he? She got up and sneaked back to the windows, peeping out. She saw no sign of Pete. She crept to the back patio door. At first she didn't see him; then she saw movement. He was digging—digging in that large landscape pot. She was mystified and riveted to the spot. She felt like shrieking, "What in the hell are you doing?" Her heart thumped like a rabbit; she was suddenly very spooked. Illiana's mind raced, but her common sense took over. She decided that whatever she had to say to him could wait until daylight. With her mind made up, she dashed to her bed, jumped in, and yanked up the covers just in time to hear the deadbolt in the kitchen.

She held her breath, afraid he might hear her. She listened to him in the bathroom. Five minutes passed, then he entered the bedroom, pulled back the covers and slid between the sheets. Quiet as a mouse, she listened. His breathing slowed into a steady patternand finally a dead snore.

At that point, she collapsed from sheer exhaustion. When she awoke later in the morning, his bed was empty. The television played in the living room. That was unusual. She got out of bed and jumped into the shower. Illiana felt she had been out on the town and had a major hangover. She allowed warm water to run over her head to erase the drugged feeling that came from crying and inadequate sleep. She had to have a hot cup of coffee. She found Pete sitting zombie-like in his big chair, tuned to the Fox channel. He had never been home in his robe on a workday in their entire marriage.

"Why are you still here? Are you taking a day off?" Receiving no answer, she continued, "I can't remember ever seeing you at home midweek in your robe."

He muttered something about needing a day off.

Her stomach sank. That would mean she couldn't get to the planter! "I'm having some toast; would you like some?" Illiana was determined to be her normal self.

"No, I don't feel like eating. I'll just stick to coffee."

She poured herself a cup from the half empty pot and dropped her bread into the toaster, never once taking her mind off last night's drama. How was she going to get a look in that planter with him in the house? She couldn't; she had to wait for the right opportunity.

Pete, to her surprise, never left the entire day. Illiana had made up her mind not to say or do anything to rock the boat. She'd just count the minutes until the coast was clear. She wanted to attack him, demand to know what he had been up to. But she was going to remain calm and do nothing to alert him to her suspicion.

Illiana mulled the entire scenario over and over in her mind; she tried desperately to make some sense of his lurking around in the motel. It was driving her crazy. She needed to speak to someone. The thought of him digging around in that big pot made her furious. She threw the towel on the counter. Now in the brightness of day, she was brave enough to confront him. There he sat in the living room, resembling a stranger. He just stared into the television. She had to get to the bottom of this and get some answers right now, the sooner the better. As she began to speak, a breaking news report interrupted the show on the television.

The reporter announced, "At ten o'clock this morning, a couple was discovered murdered in the Pecan Bend Motel. The maid found the bodies while making rounds . . ."

"Oh, my God," Illiana gasped.

Pete sat emotionless, stone faced, as if he hadn't heard the news.

Her thoughts raced. All the parts were coming together. The flashback of the events last night came full circle; this all tied in together. Illy was sure. What was she going to do? She couldn't bear anymore of this insanity; she couldn't breathe. She might be having a panic attack. She didn't know which way to turn.

Pete reached over and turned off the television and walked toward the rear of the house.

Illiana followed him. She rounded the bedroom door, expecting to see him gathering clothes to dress for work. Instead, he was crawling back into bed.

Overwhelmed and alone, she was sick, just sick. And she was sick of this queasy feeling in her stomach and of feeling afraid. She had to get to the bottom of this and soon. With a pinched voice, she managed, "Peter, what are you doing? Why are you going to bed? Are you sick?"

"Yes, shut the door and leave me alone." His tone was flat, and his back was to her.

She turned and left him, then stayed out of his way the rest of the day.

Chapter 13

It wasn't until the next morning that the old Pete reappeared. She awoke to him stirring around in the bathroom. His signature spicy fragrance filled the air. The scent was sinful, sweet, yet manly.

She got up and went to the kitchen. Deep in thought, she didn't hear Pete when he came up behind her, snaked his arm around her waist and pulled her backwards into him. He leaned forward to nuzzle her ear, and with hot breath whispered, "Sweetheart, I love you. You're the best woman I've ever known." His hands brushed over her taut breasts, sending chills over her entire body.

She responded to his warm body pressed hungrily against her. With hands on her hips, he turned her. She pivoted within the circle of his strong arms.

"Darling, thanks for being so patient with me. I know I've been difficult, but I will make up for it tonight." He kissed her fully and passionately on the lips. She drank him in, starved for his lovemaking. Her heart yielded to his words that melted her very soul. His scent intoxicated her. She was alive with that familiar desire that only he could stir in her.

He held her close and moaned while every nerve fiber in her body was titillated. She was his captive, "Pete, I love you so," she whispered huskily.

Clinging, neither wanting to let go, he gave her a final squeeze, then stood back, pecked her softly on the lips and said, "I'll see you tonight."

Illy moved to the window to see him as far as she could.

Badgering herself mentally, she wondered how she could have thought all those horrible things. Emotionally drained from the highs and lows, she needed desperately to embrace the calmness of the tender moments. She touched her finger tips to her lips recalling the feel of his soft lips on hers just moments ago. Peter slid behind the wheel. Then, horrified, she saw a veil mask his face. She was jolted back to reality. For a brief moment she'd been reunited with her love, the man she married and vowed to love forever. Illiana got caught up in the sentiment that only love creates. But it was imperative that she remain logical. She was torn by love, hate and heart-wrenching horror.

When his car disappeared, she bolted for the back yard and started slinging dirt. Her heart raced like a marathon runner. Then her arms dropped to her sides and she staggered back, barely managing to regain her balance. Tears welled in her eyes as the discovery swallowed her alive. The runaway roller coaster ran headlong into a brick wall. Stupefied, she glared straight ahead, her legs heavy. Illiana felt death all around her. She could barely make it into the house to dial the number before collapsing.

The news of the murders had been on television nonstop. The female victim was a twenty-year-old local hairdresser, and the dead man was from California. He had been living in Chapel Valley. Dixie May Sweeney was being held for questioning, but had not been charged. They televised Dixie's arrest repeatedly. The reporter mentioned there had not been a murder in Pecan Bend in over seventy-five years.

The arrest exposed Dixie at her worst; her big eyes full of fright begged for mercy.

It tore at Illiana's heart to see the poor woman so broken and pitiful, feeling all the while that she was innocent. She had to do something. She couldn't live with the gnawing ache in her stomach. Illy had to know if Peter was involved.

She recalled one day when Pete made his rounds collecting rent. He'd invited her to ride along, and when finished, they'd have dinner at the club. She took him up on it. "You've made me an offer I can't refuse."

His last stop was the Magic Touch Beauty Salon, which was directly across the parking lot from his recently relocated office. The owner of the salon was distraught when Pete mentioned the rent increase to take effect the next month.

She had fidgeted with her hair and pulled at her blouse. "The business has taken a nosedive and I can't afford an increase in rent.

Can't you take a smaller amount since I've been here for so many years?"

Pete remained stern and unyielding.

That telecast convinced Illiana that Dixie had nothing to do with those murders. If Pete were innocent, their lives would never be the same. They might never pull their marriage back together. It was a huge risk she was taking. He had been straight as an arrow until the last couple of months. He seemed dazed most of the time.

She went directly to the phone in the kitchen, not bothering to wash her hands. She asked for the detective working the case and waited for him to answer. Detective Griffin answered. They spoke for several minutes. She gave him her address, and he said he would be there in twenty minutes. Illiana Winn was a classic beauty. She sat there with her entire world upside down. She knew in her heart that the gun buried in her pot had something to do with those murders. Her gut told her so, as well as Pete's strange behavior. She knew she had reached her limit. Any decent woman worth her salt would take the same action.

When the detectives arrived, she led them to the pot. With the gun retrieved, Detective Griffin explained they would compare the bullets from the gun to the bullets that had been taken from the bodies.

Illiana looked at the lead detective. "I have to be cautious about what I say, because I don't know if my husband has anything to do with the gun or the murders in Pecan Bend. All I do know is that I saw him, and he appeared to be hiding at the motel the night of the murders."

"Go on," Detective Griffin said.

"I may be implicating Pete, and he may not have had anything to do with it." She explained that she tried speaking to Pete, and he seemed to withdraw deeper into the bizarre world in which he'd surrounded himself the last few months. "If he did it," she said, "then who were these people to him? Did he go to meet the man because he owed him money, and the girl got in the way? Too many questions are running around inside my head, and I don't have any answers."

When they were leaving, the detective stopped, looked at her, and then said, "Ma'am, we'll have an answer for you by four p.m. And, ma'am, I must ask that you not speak to anyone about this case, the gun, or any details we talked about."

She agreed and they left.

The rest of the day she kept busy performing grueling household tasks to keep her mind off the dilemma at hand. She felt her head could split with all the pressure and all the thinking she had been doing. She had to quit thinking of it for a while; she just had to. But regardless, as much as she had always loved Pete, she would not live with a killer.

She was putting her cleaning supplies back into the kitchen pantry when she saw the two detectives making their way to the side door. She knew by their faces the report was not going to be in Pete's favor. She walked to the door. Opening it, she said, "Come in."

"Ma'am, I'm afraid we have bad news for you. The bullets from the gun we found in the pot match the bullets taken from the victims."

Illiana felt the color drain from her face as the tears came. They flooded down her pretty cheeks. Her legs were so unstable she thought she might fall.

One of the detectives saw it coming. He quickly grabbed a chair and shoved it under her just in time to catch her as she went limp. She fell forward onto the tabl. Her face rested on her folded arms. That is where she stayed until she aborted the pent-up sobs held captive inside her body. She wanted to scream and rant like a crazed woman, but what good would that do? But abruptly as it started, it stopped.

She raised her swollen face. One of the detectives offered his handkerchief. He reminded her of the gentlemen of her youth. The detectives had let her cry it out very gently saying, "We are so sorry, Mrs. Winn."

She stood, walked to the kitchen sink, took a cloth, wet it and wiped her face thoroughly. When she spoke, she said, "Detectives, so what will you do now?"

They told her not to mention this to a soul, which she agreed to. They would be staked out in the neighborhood, and when they saw him come home that evening, they would immediately come, read him his rights, arrest him, and transport him to the Pecan Bend jail, where he would be charged and await trial.

    The detective said, "There won't be a bond posted; that's not feasible with murder charges." The detectives shook her hand, and with empathy they both told her how sorry they were. Detective Griffin told her that if she felt she must talk to them, to be sure and call his private cell phone. He handed her his card.

Chapter 14

Dixie May was sat in the midst of five strange women. They shared the same blank expression. The youngest of the group was still under the influence of alcohol, the reason she was arrested. Her story was, "I was driving along minding my own business when a siren blared. Flashing lights came up behind me. I was shocked to be stopped by a policeman when I was doing nothing wrong!"

Sister, Dixie thought, when you refused to be cooperative, you bought yourself a one way ticket to the slumber party at the Chapel Valley jail. But she continued to rant and Dixie thought, Woman, you're not in a good place to be ranting and raving, one of these women would just as soon give you a whipping as look at you. Dixie wanted to scream, Shut up, you fool. You're going to make it bad for everyone else!

Dixie had barely been able to choke down the bologna sandwich and dry lemon cake. When the jailer informed her of a visitor, she washed it down with some lukewarm Kool-aid. It was Jules. Jules needed information and questioned Dixie May as soon as she walked into the room. A stone-faced female officer stood in the corner. "Dixie, do you have any idea who wanted Star and Chet dead?"

"It stands to reason why they think I did it. I was jilted; my ex-boyfriend was seeing the hairdresser in my shop. I'm the woman scorned. Jules, I have racked my brain—or what's left of it—to try and figure out who did it. It's reasonable to think a jealous husband, wife, girlfriend, boyfriend, and in today's society, even a gay lover wouldn't be above suspicion."

"Were either involved in something illegal, such as drugs?"

"I don't know. Star wasn't married, and Chet is divorced, and, of course, there is me. I didn't know anything about her private life, obviously!" Dixie disclosed all the information she had and breathlessly finished, "Jules, honey, I wish I knew something to tell you about Star except the hair business. I never heard her talking to anyone. When she was at work she did hair, and she wasn't too personable with the ladies. It was common knowledge that she preferred men's company. On a few occasions when men came by, I would see a new and different Star, and that's true. But I didn't think much about it. To each their own, I've always said. I don't nose around in anyone's affairs unless they point blank asked me a question."

Jules sat back in her chair, tapping her pencil on the arm of the chair.

They talked for ten more minutes, then Jules said she was meeting Joy and Jettie at her office. The guard came to escort Dixie out. "I can assure you I will not leave a stone unturned," Jules said. The ladies hugged and said goodbye.

Jules rushed into the lobby, her arms overloaded. She looked the part of an accomplished businesswoman in a gray fitted suit with straight hair that swung to her high cheekbones and back as she moved. She was a walking advertisement. Who wouldn't want her representing their law firm? Joy and Jettie followed her into her office. The entire back wall was appointed with impressive leather-bound law books. Jules allowed her shoulder bag to slide onto the table, then wrestled the heavy black attaché case onto the massive mahogany desk. Still standing, she clicked the case open. Then she sat in the winged back chair and announced, "Ladies, Dixie May has herself in a very hot spot."

Joy and Jettie both nodded, and then Joy said, "Yes, but, what is she going to do? What can we do to help?"

Jules removed a stack of papers from her case. Adjusting her glasses, she read from her notes. "I've hired Kasi King, one of the top private investigators in Texas, to perform background checks on all parties in this case, the suspect, and the victims. Furthermore, I want her to dig up anyone who had grievances or any reason to kill either or both of the slain. Kasi will start digging into Dixie's whereabouts, who she has been spending her time with for the last thirty days. I further instructed my assistant, Jon Roy, to engage the services of Dr. Avery and his staff to counsel Dixie, then evaluate her mental state. I will need a written report filed with the court the day trial begins, assuming there will be a trial." She returned the papers to the case. Then folding her hands on her desk, she said, "That's all we can do at this time."

Jules leaned back in her chair. "I'll do the best I can for Dixie May. We'll save her from the death sentence."

Joy reached over to comfort Jettie, and the old friends embraced.

The phone rang, startling Joy. She hurried to answer it. "I'm on my way to the Chapel Valley jail," Jules said. "Dixie May is being released. Dr. Avery said it would be best for her to stay at your place or Jettie's tonight. Then she can check into Timber Lawn early tomorrow. Dr. Avery said she needs twenty-four/seven supervision."

"Do you want me to ride with you, or what?" Joy asked.

"No, Chauncey is already with me, so you won't have to go out. Dr. Avery took care of all the pre-admission red tape for Dixie May. All she has to do is check in, and they will assign her a room."

"Okay, then," Joy said, "bring Dixie May here, and I'll get her bed ready." She drummed on the table. "I have to call Jettie and everyone waiting to hear this news."

"Okay, Mom, I'll see you soon."

As soon as she hung up, Joy rang Jettie, talking fifty miles a minute. "They are about to release Dixie May. And Jules thought it best for Dixie to stay at my house or yours. Dr. Avery said she would need twenty-four/seven monitoring until she was mentally evaluated. And he wants her admitted to Timber Lawn in the morning. He'll make all the necessary arrangements. All we need to do is gather her personal items."

Jettie was elated. "I'll stay here and call everyone about the release." She and Joy planned to meet at Joy's in the morning.

Camilla messaged Jettie daily. She was well-informed on the case and all the details. Krystal and Johnny were faithful and offered to do whatever they could to help.

Toby told Jettie, "I ran into a buddy at breakfast this morning at the local coffee shop, and he told me that Chet's children and ex-wife had checked into the Willow Motel. And they said they plan to sit and make sure their dad got justice, and the murderer got what she deserved—the death sentence."

"That's not the first time I've heard that," Jettie said.

Pecan Bend hadn't been the same since the first day the murder was discovered, and it would probably be a long time before they quit talking about it. In the evening, most families were glued to the television for any tidbit of news related to the murders. They got more than a tidbit that night. A breaking news report stated another suspect had been arrested for the double murder. The city of Pecan Bend was mayhem, with cops, reporters and spectators crowding the streets. The city was feeling the whiplash of two arrests made within two days of the double murder. A local man had been arrested, positively identified, and charged. The media reported the residents were getting paranoid. They were clamoring for justice. They wanted to add more police or do whatever it took to protect the public.

There would be more information on the ten p.m. news. The police issued a curfew and urged all residents to stay off the streets unless they had business to attend.

Dixie was released from jail and admitted to Timber Lawn the following morning per Dr. Phillip Avery's instructions. Dr. Rodney Wallace, a longtime friend and associate of Dr. Avery's, specialized in women's mental health issues, and Dr. Avery felt confident that he was the one to work with Dixie May.

Timber Lawn was an old facility, but still beautiful. Fine art adorned the walls of the admittance area, and rich hardwood floors greeted the visitors. The waiting areas were plush with rich hunter green carpet and the walls elegantly designed with a deep swirled effect in neutral hues. It created an easy ambiance, key for the patients living within the compound. The large area was enhanced with custom seating built in a wrap-around fashion attached to the walls. A black baby grand Baldwin graced the center of the room, making a bold yet stately presentation. Forty people could easily be accommodated at visitation. It was a special treat to sit and listen to the pianist during the "Ivory Hour." It was exactly what the doctor ordered. The tranquility inspired an atmosphere of healing.

"You forget you are in a mental facility when you walk into this elegant foyer," Joy said.

Jettie was curious about the music room and dismissed herself to go investigate. As usual, Jettie returned with abundant news. Between the hours of two and four, Dr. Wallace arranged for a pianist to play for the patients and visiting families. Jettie was impressed. "What a lovely gesture, and how wise of this doctor."

Dr. Rodney Wallace visited Dixie the first day, and then twice a week in one-hour sessions. She would be on the couch, he in his chair, as she spoke from the depths of her heart. The session ended with his evaluation of her thoughts and responses. Dixie soon had a better understanding of her behavior with the opposite sex. Dr. Wallace reported she was doing remarkably well. Jettie and Joy visited Dixie weekly and often stopped by Dr. Wallace's office for a report. They were treated as Dixie May's family, since Dixie declared no close relatives.

Chapter 15

As a child, Dixie was forever overachieving to impress her demanding mother, but she never succeeded. Her mother made endless remarks such as, "You should have," or "Why didn't you?"

When Dr. Wallace and Dixie talked of those times, Dixie remembered the way she felt as she lay in her bed and heard her mother talk on the phone to her sisters, making statements like, "No, she didn't make it; that pretty little girl won."

"I would bury my face in my pillow and fill it with tears," Dixie said. "I was a little girl trapped in a fantasy world. I dreamed of winning a beauty contest so Mother would be proud of me. Or I would be a movie star, and Mother would be right there with the cameras flashing. People would shout, 'You did such a good job.' And she would boast, 'Yes, she's my beautiful princess.'"

Every session was better than the last. Dixie was radiant within a few weeks.

On another of Dixie's sessions they delved further into her childhood. Dr. Wallace pointed out how she developed her relations with boys. It was a direct result of the dysfunctional relationship with her mother. She had given up trying to please her mother years before, finally realizing that would never happen. Her behavior was formed and the cycle began and would be forever present. She could remember even as an eleven-year-old having her first boyfriend, Gary, in the fifth grade. He sat in the row beside her. He presented her with a little bracelet. She mimicked what she saw the older girls do. She had to be the cutest girl, with the cutest smile, saying the cutest things, and speaking in the softest little voice.

Dr. Wallace explained she was repeating the behavior she had learned while living with her mother—to do or say whatever it took to please, to be the best, to win. She had many boyfriends through junior high, high school, adulthood and finally one failed marriage after another, resulting in the decision to remain single for the past twelve years.

"When you became afraid, no longer willing to feel the pain that went with a relationship, you played safe and blocked yourself from being accessible to others. You were in self-preservation mode, since you had been hurt too many times in the past. You were no longer willing to allow yourself to be vulnerable." Dr. Wallace kept talking until she had to listen and allow his words to penetrate.

Dixie understood perfectly what he had said. And it was all true. Dixie felt the yoke had been removed, and she was free from the heavy load, reborn and free as the birds in the sky. She was invigorated to know she was not a lost cause; there was hope for her.

Dr. Wallace was an exceptional doctor. Dixie found herself wondering if he was married. He was a good-looking, charming man. He apparently worked out. She saw no fat on his medium frame. She'd noticed him many times in the gardens. He read a book after lunch and appeared to be a calm, pleasant man. His love for the outdoors accounted for his tanned arms and legs. Dixie didn't see how he ever made time for pleasure—he was at the hospital day in and day out. If he had a significant other, she must be an angel to put up with his hours.

Off in her own thoughts, she managed to reel herself back for his question. "In a nutshell, it's up to you. Do you want a better life, to find true happiness, or do you see yourself continuing on the same road?"

"There is no way I want to continue on the same old road!" she said. "That's why I'm here—to do whatever it takes to fix my problem. I want victory over my problem, because, Dr. Wallace, I hope to laugh and love and dance 'til the cows come home!"

He grinned, not having a clue what that statement meant, but she said it with enthusiasm and that is what counted. She was loving and fun. He was delighted to spend the day with her. The largest percent of the time she was happy with the most explosive outbursts of laughter he had ever heard. "Okay, Dixie, that's it for today; I'm ready to throw in the towel. How about you?"

"Yes, sir." She had nothing to do but twiddle her thumbs or walk in the garden and visit with people. Dixie May, with Dr. Wallace's help, would never be imprisoned by her ignorance again.

Dr. Rodney Wallace and Dr. Phillip Avery discussed Dixie May's progress. Rodney thought she was well on the way to recovery. It was critical that she stay on the medication therapy for at least a year to maintain a good chemical balance, and then he would meet her twice a year to see if she needed a change. She had greatly improved over the last month and was not at all like that frantic woman they'd brought in. Her appearance was understandable, given the way she had been handled and slammed in a jail cell. Being interrogated for the murders of the two people had done a number on her. She'd come such a long way in such a short time. She truly had a new lease on life. There was a bounce in her step. She was a regular chitty-chatty gal.

Dr. Avery was delighted to receive such a glowing report and said he'd convey the information to Joy Hillary and Jettie McNamara.

Dr. Wallace asked, "Why are they considered, since they aren't family? I must have overlooked something; I know she has a sister."

"Dixie signed a release form at my office authorizing them as closest of kin. Seems her parents are both deceased and nobody knows where the sister lives. These women have been friends all their lives."

"That's good to know," Dr. Wallace said. "I've been intending to ask. I'll note that on her file."

Chapter 16

Dr. Wallace sat in his plush office with pecan plantation shutters, hunter green carpet, burgundy leather sofa and chair, full desk with a wall of books, and a huge aquarium of large exotic fish with bright colors. Schools of fish swam back and forth. It was lovely, with rocks, greenery and a sunken Titanic lodged at the bottom. The fish darted in and out of the portholes. It was tranquilizing. Definitely a man's office, with the lovely lingering smell of the woman, he thought as he sniffed the air to capture the scent she left behind. She mystified him. Sitting there feeling her presence, her voice rang in his ears. He'd never thought of a patient as anything but a patient, but Dixie stirred feelings that were foreign to him. He was drawn to her like he had no will of his own. And he knew better than to allow these feelings—feelings that seemed to have gotten stronger in the last few days.

Rodney stood. He tried to will away the intense feelings. Walking to the cooler, he drew a cup of water. It was in Dixie's best interest that she was willing to change. She yearned for a good and happy life. Being so vibrant and full of energy, he could see how the men in her life had been attracted to her. She had allowed Chet Tyler, the dead man, into her life and truly believed him to be the man of her dreams. He apparently swept her off her feet. She had been vigilant for twelve long years. That man had sucked her in. She was full of life. What was not to like? No wonder men chased her. Rodney shook his head. Well, some men. Dixie was a typical Southern woman and proud of her heritage. He concluded that she was on the road to recovery. She desired balance and self-respect in her life.

According to his original plan, Dr. Avery wanted Dixie to stay two months at Timber Lawn. She had only one month left in the hospital. He mulled it over, and considering that Phillip wanted her there for a sixty-day run, Rodney decided to honor his recommendation and let her finish up, get stronger, and have time to put all the distressing news of the murder and trial away. At least that would give her another month, hopefully time for all the chaos in Pecan Bend to blow over. His decision made, he stood, stretched, gathered up his jacket and briefcase, then headed to the door.

At the Enchanted Gardens Tea Room, Camilla, Krystal, Joy and Jettie passed on having wine. They decided to wait for Dixie's return, and then they would celebrate with a special bottle that Camilla would bring from Italy. They ordered the basics and counted their blessings. After lunch and a little chit chat, they headed to Dallas.

They were going to surprise Dixie May with an unannounced visit and tea beneath the shade of the lush oak branches in Timber Lawn's garden. Camilla had flown in from Houston, and Krystal had left Johnny to fend for himself. The girls needed to catch up, pull in, and come together. Joy said a heart-to-heart session was overdue, so she had organized a special get together for the circle of friends. The ladies agreed they would do what they did best, and that was love Dixie back to wellness. The tea party would be fun and so typical of the circle of friends, a real girly-girl thing.

Dr. Wallace was expecting them. At Joy's request, he promised to drop by and meet all the ladies. Jettie was furnishing Chai, a hot oriental spiced tea she liked to serve with honey and amaretto cream. She packed it into a white wicker basket along with fine china, delicate napkins, embroidered tablecloth, and scones to nibble with the tea.

Dixie was elated, squealing like a young girl, when she saw them with their faces pressed against her bedroom window, where she was writing in her journal. She jumped up and ran out to meet them. They hugged and cheek kissed, then linked arms and started down to "Tranquility"—the special place they liked to meet under the tree. The girls had really surprised her. When the doctor stopped by, he sat and joined them for tea. He was a pleasant surprise for the other girls, who were impressed with him as a man and a fine doctor.

Camilla remarked that she thought he was so cool because of his willingness to drink tea, putting aside the fact that he was the doctor. They all felt Dixie was in excellent hands, and went on to say that he seemed genuinely interested in her, maybe more so than just a doctor. Krystal smiled, always being the romantic.

Dixie said, "He's my favorite doctor, and he treats me as if I'm his only patient."

Dr. Wallace agreed, knowing it was the truth. He had not been aware that his feelings were so obvious, but he would make a point to be more conscious of his demeanor when in her presence.

Back in his office and alone, the doctor pondered his situation. He latched his door; he wanted time to think undisturbed. Money was never a problem for him; it simply sat in the bank drawing interest. He had no one, no demands, no hobbies to drain his finances. One might find him a trifle dull. Ambitious women jumped at the opportunity to be escorted by such a celebrated doctor. He was not so naive that he didn't realize what went on in the real world.

Last week he found himself searching for Dixie on the grounds. He wanted to hear her voice, listen to her talk and use her hands when she became excited and see that huge Texas smile spread when she was happy. He loved her Southern charm and Southern drawl; there was no pretense—she was herself in any situation. It was truly fascinating and refreshing to him. He had feelings for her that sent deeper than just doctor and patient.

Time was getting away. In fact, he hadn't been able to remember what he'd done before her arrival a few short weeks ago. He had never been so electrified by a woman's presence.

Chapter 17

Never had Pecan Bend been like this, and it probably never would be again.

The arrested man had admitted committing the murders. He wrote a lengthy letter admitting his guilt and gave graphic details of the executions.

> March 5, 2005
> *Daily News Telegram*
> Pecan Bend, Texas
>
> Peter Winn's handwritten confession:
>
> She convinced me that I was different, told me she loved me. I was a sucker and bought it. At first I felt sorry for her when she told me how bad her life had been. She had no use for women, she fixed their hair but she worked them to get to know their men. She did sexual favors for money, things the men couldn't get at home. They begged for more. She told me they were old geezers with their shriveled up old bodies and they made her want to barf. She loved describing the details to make me jealous. When I got jealous, she went wild. She was a freak. She was quicksand sucking me under. I was obsessed with her. I called her that last day and told her I wanted to marry her. I told her I was going to get a divorce. She laughed hysterically. She screamed, "Get a grip, Petey, it's good while it lasts! You are making me sick. You sound like one of those old geezers." Then she slammed the phone down. At one point I moved my office across from the

beauty shop so I could spy on her. The guilt ate me alive. I wasn't the same man. She was like crystal meth, and she drove me crazy. I wasn't able to look at myself in the mirror. I thought about cutting my throat, but didn't have the guts. The day she laughed and called me an old geezer and hung up was the day I knew I was going to kill her. I knew where to find her; all I had to do was wait. Sure enough, she was shacked up with another low life. I walked in and they didn't even know I was there. They were too busy pawing and panting. She opened those baby blues and looked at me over his shoulder and stared down the nose of my 38. I pulled the trigger, then I put a bullet in the back of his head. The pawing and panting stopped. They deserved to die. Sooner or later somebody would've killed them. When you jerk people around, it's inevitable.

Even though she was doing great, Dr. Avery felt it best to keep Dixie in the facility for the final week.

Then she would be gone forever. Her laughter would no longer resonate in the courtyard.

Dr. Wallace arrived early the next morning. He entered the office, coffee in hand, humming as he walked. Without looking, he tossed the mail onto his desk. He went to the window, opened the shutters, and let the sun filter in.

Returning to the desk, a return address on the large, impressive envelope caught his eye. He grabbed the letter opener, slit it open and pulled out a crisp white letter with an engraved letterhead, New York Presbyterian Psychiatry Hospital.

Immediately sitting, he began to read.

Dear Dr. Wallace,

You have been selected to visit us in New York at the NYPH to discuss a position that has just become available. Your years of dedication to the field of psychiatry are impressive. Your many awards speak volumes about your ability and character.

Due to a health situation, Dr. Marcus Stanley is retiring a few months early. We are seeking his replacement, and that is the reason we are contacting you. We would like for you to fly at our expense to check out our beautiful facilities and campus. The position available is Executive Director of our Columbia Division of NYPH. Please reply as soon as possible.

Cordially,
Glyndale Gilbert
Executive V.P. of Operations

It felt good; unexpected but flattering. He had to admit it was thrilling to even be considered for such a position. He'd been fortunate to complete his education in Texas and spend thirty-five years of his career in one location. Yes, he was interested. It perked his spirits greatly.

NYPH was one of the top three psychiatric hospitals in the nation, and they had notified him. Woo Hoo! He was honored. Only needing to think on it a few minutes, he knew he would accept the invitation to check it out. It would be wise to keep his options open.

Dixie May walked into view, feminine, easy on the eyes. Not wanting to miss the opportunity, he poured more coffee and walked in her direction.

When he caught up with her, she said, "Good morning, Doctor." They chit chatted about trivial matters. He told her he enjoyed visiting with her girlfriends.

She looked at him. "They are special to me, like sisters."

They sat under the oaks until it was time for his first session. On impulse, he asked, "Dixie, have you ever been to New York City?"

Before answering, she tossed a little seed to the waiting birds. "Heavens, no. I've hardly been out of Texas. Doctor, my whole life has been about work and paying bills; there was no time for adventure."

"I'm going to go to New York in a few weeks. Remind me to tell you about my trip."

"I'll be sure and do that. See you in the morning, Doc."

Dixie knew that these conversations were between Rodney and Dixie, not doctor and patient. They had become friends, and she liked that. He was a good man. She took out the book she brought to read after her walk, opened it, and lay back in one of the garden recliners. What a life, she thought, you can't beat this.

Krystal followed Johnny around the yard. He was spring-cleaning—straightening up and stretching the tarp over the boat. They'd been living in the same home for nearly forty years. Krystal called it her dream home. Many a garden party had been held there— they lived to entertain. Both were extremely social and spent the major part of their lives with friends, keeping a full calendar. Usually they favored cruises around the islands on romantic getaways or rode their Harley with a members group. Many trips took them to the country in southwest Texas. Tourists flocked there to swim or river raft in the Guadalupe. Krystal loved to say, "I'm a Harley Honey."

They had been spending more time at home. Several important events were on the horizon, so Johnny had to catch up on his "honey do" list.

Krystal had talked to Joy earlier about Dixie and her therapy. "Dixie will be released soon and will be back to her old self," Joy said. "She discussed some tentative plans for the salon, which mainly means she doesn't have a plan." Joy understood her to say the shop was secure for a while, since the rent and utilities were paid. "She said that when she reopened, it would take some time to rebuild her clientele."

"It might be a good idea to tell Dixie to discuss that with Dr. Wallace."

They said good night and hung up the phones. Krystal went to find Johnny in the backyard. He had the grill ready to sizzle the steaks to perfection. "Darling," he said, "would you bring those big boys out of the fridge; they're marinating. And as soon as I get them, your daddy will get your dinner on the table."

Krystal, enjoying the role-play, teased back, "Well, tell me, handsome, what's for dessert?" He chuckled and pinched her on her back porch when she swished away.

Later, over their steaks, Krystal said, "Can you believe Vince and Joy are marrying after all this time?"

"True love, baby," he answered. "I hope all of our out-of-town travel is arranged. Have you secured our flights and hotel to Tahoe? We can't wait too late; it wouldn't be fun with no place to sleep."

Walking silently into the house, she decided she'd better double check—she couldn't remember. If she'd forgotten, Johnny would never let her live it down.

Krystal felt better once she checked her desk and found the reservation information. She had just forgotten to put it in her day timer.

The wedding date was Saturday, April 7, at four p.m.

Krystal came back and took a seat on the sofa, where Johnny watched a sports event. "We'll fly out on Friday, April 6, at 10:00 a.m., and fly home on Monday, April 9, at 9:00 p.m.."

"You are making the plans, dear; I'll be ready when you are."

Lake Tahoe would be breathtaking in the spring and a perfect setting for a wedding, especially right smack in the middle of the resort with forty friends.

Jettie and Joy had outdone themselves on the affair. They loved to plan special events. This was definitely in the top two ever. The wedding would be formal, the bride in the traditional white gown and the groom in a white tux with tails. They would be aboard the Blue Wave Yacht for two hours. The forty-five-foot white yacht was reserved for the wedding at Zephyr Cove. Invitations had been mailed to their closest friends and family. The ceremony would be thirty minutes, and the rest of the time would be spent on photos, cake, and socializing. Camilla and Rocky would surprise the newlyweds with a special gift. The secret was killing Jettie.

Jettie and Toby had to return to Texas right after the wedding. They had business to tend to and could not avoid it. Ben would be their personal pilot. All Jettie had to do was relax in the small plane. That could be hard to do. "She isn't your best passenger, but she isn't a white knuckler," Toby had been known to say.

The reception would be at Squaw Valley Resort. The hotel where the newlyweds would spend their honeymoon night was close by. The resort had mountain access as well as a white sandy beach—the best of both worlds. The next day Vince would drive his bride to their beautiful Truckee home, and it would be there Vince would carry his wife across the threshold.

Chapter 18

Back in Texas, the doctor grew fonder of Dixie with each passing day. He felt he'd known her forever. They met in the morning for a brisk walk, then he would leave her to begin his day. Release day approached. He admitted his selfishness. She had no reason to continue in the institution, other than allowing time to let the trial settle down in Chapel Valley. Just the mere mention of her departure made him miss her. At times it surprised him that nobody seemed to notice all the attention he gave her, that nothing had been mentioned.

Rodney sat behind his desk, pondering the last several days and thinking of his future. He whirled his chair backwards, scrunching down; he worked a rubber band around his fingers and stared at the wall full of books. It dawned on him what he was doing—he was saying his goodbyes to his surroundings, he was letting go. It grew clearer—he wanted change. Three days had passed since he received the New York letter, and he had to give them an answer in two days. He desperately wanted to check it out, but he was drawn in two different directions—New York and this crazy sensation that he hated to leave Dixie. He had never been affected by a woman in this way. And it was crazy, he knew. She would be leaving the institution in just a few days, but she was constantly on his mind. He was toying with the idea of asking her to join him on the trip.

She lay on the couch and talked. "I have decided to sell the salon. With all the bad press, I think it would be wiser for me to relocate to another town." She had a lot of decisions to make.

From his swivel chair, he peered at her over his glasses. "I agree. I don't think it would be best for you to return to the salon; the gossip will last forever. And, knowing your history, I agree it would be best to move to Silver Springs where you have friends. But ultimately, of course, that decision is one you will have to make."

In between patients, Rodney thought about the New York trip; there was a lot to see in five nights. He would have full eight-hour days at the hospital. He logged in to the net to search hotels and sights to see, plays to attend. His anticipation mounted. Rodney lined up the lovely attractions to visit, but his timing must be right on the money to invite her along. The most exciting aspect was the possibility of Dixie accompanying him. They had a suite available for her at the Waldorf, down the hall from his. He planned to make it perfectly clear that Dixie would have separate quarters, no strings attached.

He knew she had no money to waste on extravagance at this time. He would give her money to spend on Madison and Park Avenues. When he returned to the hotel in the afternoon, they could stroll in Central Park and look for giant oaks like the ones in Texas. Rodney couldn't wait to see her face when they drove from the airport to the hotel, taking in Times Square. He couldn't think of anyone he'd rather put on a pedestal than this little Southern belle.

He repeated the credit card number to the agent and then hung up; wanting to surprise Dixie, he had booked a Broadway play. She told him she dreamed of riding the buggy in Central Park and visiting the Metropolitan Museum of Art. If she said no, he would just have to cancel, but at least he'd be prepared.

Rodney nervously fiddled with his pen and doodled on the scratch pad. Finally, Glyndale Gilbert answered. He got right to the point and told her to expect him at the end of the week. She was nice, but definitely a Yankee. He was amused by her thick New York accent. It further amused him to think he sounded like a country hick to her. Rodney might look many things, but icky hicky he was not. He was groomed to perfection, toned and tanned. He religiously worked out three times a week at home. The coveted full head of dark brown hair was his crowning glory. It was now laced with strands of silver over his ears and sprinkles throughout, giving him a distinguished look. Every few years he'd try out a new mustache, wear it through the winter, and trim it off in the spring. He looked good either way, probably younger without, some of his lady friends had remarked.

He went home and retired for the night. He tried to sleep, but instead, tossed and turned, punching his pillow. When he raised his head for the tenth time to peek at the clock, slivers of golden sun peeked through the tiny slits of the blinds. He felt the adrenalin rush when his feet hit the floor. He took a speedy shower, jumped in the car, and sped away to the hospital. He didn't even bother with breakfast. Today was the day. She would either say yes or no, and he would have to deal with the consequences. He was on a mission, and he wanted to hear that one little word—yes—and then his feet wouldn't hit the ground for the rest of the day. He did work in a regular cup of java. Mandy, his personal assistant, made it for him every morning, rain or shine. She'd been the office coordinator for five years and he didn't know what he would do without her. If the New York job worked out, he'd be finding out. So much was up in the air about his future. He wondered how other people handled moving every few years.

He had finished his second cup when he got a glimpse of Dixie headed to the oaks. He stood and waited, making sure that was her destination. It was. He went out the door with the most important question he'd ever had to ask in his personal life. He felt like he was in puberty and about to ask for his first date. He would have to be delicate. After all, he was her doctor and still in charge and responsible for her care. And he didn't want to spook her and make her think he was up to one thing. That was the furthest thing from his mind.

She saw him coming and moved over on the bench. "Want to sit?" she asked.

"Not right now. Come on. Let's walk."

"Okay, you're the doc." She smiled, a little amused with what she'd said.

They enjoyed each other's company and chatted about how their nights had gone and what she had planned for the day. Dixie had begun to paint a couple of weeks earlier, a passion from her past. Rodney noticed her sketching flowers and mentioned it to her. She told him it had been a passion, but she had to give it up due to time. "After working all week I was too tired to allow myself to be consumed, and that's easily done with art."

"Remember me mentioning the job offer?" he said.

"Yes."

He motioned for her to sit. She did, and staring at him, waited for his reply.

"Now, Dixie, you know that we have become more than doctor and patient. We have bonded as friends. Do you agree?"

She nodded.

"And we've talked about much more than your health."

She nodded again, a bit puzzled as to where this was headed.

His face turned serious. "Dixie, I'm going to accept their offer to go for the interview. I'm excited about it in a way I've never been before in my career. But, here's the problem. First of all, I know this may shock you, but I would like for you to join me and see Manhattan while we have the chance. It wouldn't cost you a penny. I will pay for everything. They're paying my way, but I don't want to go it alone in New York. I don't think that would be much fun."

He took a deep breath. "And whatever you're thinking—put it out of your mind. You'll have your suite and I'll have mine. When I'm at the hospital, you can do whatever you like. Then at night, we can do the city." He told her he had to call them the next day.

She was astonished. She had never dreamed of such a thing. "Doctor, I'm speechless. That's a whole lot to think about."

"I know."

"What would people say?"

"I'd rather they didn't know. It would be frowned upon, with you being a patient."

She stood. "I'm going to mull this over and I'll get back to you. How soon do you need an answer?"

"By four tomorrow," he answered.

"I'll see you here at three-thirty."

With that, she was off. Her imagination ran wild. All this was overwhelming; it just racked her mind. It was a once in a lifetime opportunity. Travel with him; what did that mean? Could she trust him? Did he want her to just keep him company? She knew they were becoming more than doctor and patient. Knowing he was breaking the doctor-patient relationship rule puzzled her. He was such a dedicated man. Why would he take such a risk? He was undoubtedly the nicest man she ever knew, and he was an educated man. It didn't get much better than that. He was a man of character.

She could see all of New York, and it wouldn't cost her a dime. He would put her up in her own room. She was going! She felt giddy. It had been a long time since she'd taken a trip.

She woke up that morning and counted the hours, then minutes for the time to meet him again, and now the time had arrived. It was three-fifteen p.m. and Dixie May was a new woman. She could hardly walk at a normal pace; she wanted to run to meet Rodney. She felt she had known this man forever. Last night, she had written out all the pros and cons regarding the trip, and the pros won. She decided it would be the best thing for her.

Chapter 19

Rodney sat on the bench, not knowing whether to be happy or sad, not knowing what Dixie May's decision would be. He was intelligent enough to think about the negative side and what he would do if she turned him down. It made him sad to think that he could be alone in a big city packed with strangers. Ultimately, he'd pull it together if the offer was anywhere close to what he anticipated.

Deep in thought, he didn't see Dixie May until she stood over him. Blinded by the sun, he looked up. Managing to make out her smile, he knew all he needed to know. When she sat down, her dress stirred a soft powdery fragrance that was as lovely as the woman. He breathed it in, wanting to wrap his arms around her and smother her with kisses. Instead, he smiled at her with his mouth as well as his eyes; then he winked to let her know what he could not say. People were always outside and walking around. It was such a beautiful lush courtyard that the only time people did not migrate to it was in the cold of winter.

"Doctor, I want to make sure you understand I can't pay for anything, not even my meals. When I don't work, my ship returns to sea." She just smiled. "If it's a problem, then I won't be doing New York." She wanted to get it out; now she had. She looked at him, waiting.

"Lady, just like I told you yesterday, it will be completely my treat—you don't have to worry that pretty red head about anything. I'll take care of all the arrangements; just pack your suitcases for a week's stay and we'll have a wonderful time."

The plans were made. It was decided. When she checked out of the hospital, they would drive to DFW, connect with American Airlines, and fly directly into LaGuardia, then hail a taxi to the Waldorf. He had reservations, to which she replied, "Hah, what if I'd said no?"

He answered, "I really wanted you to go, but they assured me all I had to do was cancel."

"What am I going to wear? My clothes are eighty miles east of here!"

"I've already thought of that. There are many boutiques around the Waldorf within walking distance. But not to worry. We can stop by North Park on the way to the airport and pick you up a few things at Neiman's. Do you think a couple of cocktail dresses, shoes, jewelry, casual attire and intimate apparel, would take care of it?"

She was flattered and flabbergasted. Dixie nodded. She had never had a man cater to her in such a manner.

"We don't want anyone to know of our adventure. So going to Chapel Valley isn't possible, if our plans are to remain hush-hush. You know we would be spotted."

"Well, that's true enough." She thought all the secrecy made it doubly exciting.

He looked at his watch. "I'd love to stay and make more plans, but I must get back. A session begins in fifteen minutes." He reached over and squeezed her hand, then rose to leave.

She stood. She absolutely could not believe this. She knew how Cinderella must have felt. Laughing, she had never met a man like him in her entire life. She was thrilled with the opportunity to explore New York City, escorted by this distinguished gentleman. It still had not sunk in. Who would have thought it? Of all places to meet a man, she thought this one was for the books. She strolled, clinging to the glorious feeling of being important to someone, desired by a man who demanded nothing in return.

Friday arrived, and Dixie May was dressed and ready to check out. The nurse had been down to her room to have her sign release forms. Dixie walked to the window to take a final look at Tranquility. It filled her with serenity. During her stay, she had sat under the trees and watched little birds eager to peck the breadcrumbs as she tossed them to the ground. The oak branches rocked with the breeze and the leaves rustled.

She rolled her bag down the hall to the front door. She made her goodbye simple and waved. Dixie May was leaving a different woman than the woman who entered this place the dreadful day of her check in. Once outside, she drew in the fresh air and filled her lungs. She felt God smiled down on her and had sent the sun to shine especially for her while she walked back into the world to make her fresh start. And he had sent this special man to her, she thought, as she spied the shiny black Mercedes parked where he promised it would be. Her heart skipped a beat. He opened the door as she approached and stepped out to greet her and handle her baggage. The two of them never knew what was ahead of them, but they knew they had strong feelings and trusted each other explicitly.

They got in the car feeling like two teenagers on the sneak. He reached over and squeezed her knee, and she felt a flutter in the pit of her stomach.

"I cannot believe I'm on the way to New York City," she said.

He took her hand. "Well, you are, my dear. Right along with me. We will board in four hours and arrive in Manhattan at seven tonight."

"This is too good to be true."

"We'll stop at Neiman's and be there a couple of hours," Rodney said. "How about a quick bite in their restaurant, then we can have a late dinner in the city?"

"That sounds wonderful."

"You'll probably be tired and want to rest by then. We're booked in first class, so that should allow us room enough to stretch out and catch a few winks before we land."

"You're the man, Doc." Then she smiled that big smile that created deep dimples in each cheek

At Neiman's, he sat patiently and waited for her to model each outfit. He motioned her to turn, then offered his opinion. It gave her a shot of self esteem and reminded her she was a desired woman. The first dress was ivory with layers of chiffon, a full skirt made for dancing, which she demonstrated with a whirl. Rodney laughed. She circled and walked back and forth for him, stopping to look at him over her shoulder with her hand on her hip, and said, fluttering her eyelashes, "Well, so what do you think?" The strapless heels flattered her creamy calves.

The doctor nodded his head and drawled, "Maybe."

She left only to return in a black spaghetti strap dress, which accentuated her tiny waist and hugged her curves in all the right places. Again she pranced and posed, and the doctor seemed to like this one much better. He said, "I believe that is a possibility." His favorite was a red cocktail mini-dress with studded jacket and a fitted red belt with studded buckle. It had a plunging neckline with a built-in bustier, which she wore with clear evening slippers. She carried a tiny studded evening bag.

"Dixie dear, I believe you should have all three dresses and the Armani pantsuits."

She selected several other items such as sleepwear and undergarments, and a lounging jacket to wear for dinner on the terrace, if she were in the mood. He bought her everything she even glanced at, and some things he just thought she should have, as well as a designer travel bag set. When the clerk rang up the bill, Rodney pulled out his credit card and didn't blink an eye when the total was over $3,000. After all, they were at Neiman's.

The clerk packed the luggage with the purchases. Rodney pulled the large one while Dixie pulled the other. He grabbed her loose hand and held it while they made their way to the parking lot. Everything fit snugly in the trunk of the Mercedes. Not only did he have to buy her clothes, he purchased luggage to carry it all, she thought with amusement. Well, if it was okay with him, it was okay with her.

Their timing was perfect. They arrived at the airport, the bags were loaded, and they boarded the plane. Their flight was on time, and soon after they settled into their spacious first-class seats, the pilot announced, "We are right on schedule. The weather in New York is clear and warm, making for a marvelous visit to the Big Apple. So enjoy your flight, and come fly again with us at American."

Everything about Manhattan was huge. Dixie was breathless except for the oohs and ahhs when she recognized streets and buildings.

She reminded Rodney of a Texas rose in full bloom. She was radiant; he couldn't take his eyes off her. That big smile lit up her face. Lord, the woman made him happy.

When the driver pulled up in front of the Waldorf Astoria, Dixie just stared; the architecture was amazing. The uniformed doorman walked to the taxi, opened her door, and summoned a bellhop to carry the bags. At the registration desk, Dixie gazed around, trying not to be obvious, but she was captivated with the finery of the massive rooms—the famous art collection, lush designer walls, high rotunda ceilings, and marble flooring.

They were soon on their way up to the fourteenth floor, escorted by the bellhop, who swung open two double doors to a luscious room with fireplace and a balcony overlooking Central Park. The bellhop put her clothes away and opened the French doors to the balcony to let in fresh air.

The carpeting was at least three inches deep, white and fluffy. Dixie took off her shoes and walked barefoot in it, while the bellhop led Rodney to his adjoining suite, just as he had promised. She circled the room, wrapped her arms around herself and squeezed. Giggling, she ran to the bedroom and jumped in the middle of the giant bed made for royalty. "Oh my," she said out loud, "I could live here forever and never leave this room."

Dixie ran a bath and poured a generous amount of bath oil in the water. She pinned up her hair and wrapped a towel around her body. She went to call Rodney's room and tell him that she would be ready to go to dinner in an hour. He didn't have to go to the hospital until early Monday morning, so they had the entire weekend to explore the city. He made reservations in Peacock Alley, the restaurant centered in the hotel. They decided to stay close to the hotel that night, since it had been a big day. They planned to sit on her terrace later and admire the New York skyline while sharing a few glasses of wine.

The suite was more like a luxurious apartment than a suite; it had a living room with a white marble fireplace, a bedroom with sitting area, a dressing room off the palatial bath and dressing area, breakfast area with fridge, a study with desk and laptop and internet access. The bath had wall-to-wall mirrors and marble floors; the faucet in the tub was a long-necked brass swan head; the water flowed from the swan's mouth. The Jacuzzi jets kept the bubbles bouncing and bubbling about the tub as Dixie lounged full length in it. She thought how very lucky she had been to meet Rodney. She couldn't believe that some cute thing hadn't taken him off the market years ago. But, in remembering a previous conversation, he made it perfectly clear that he had no intention of looking for a woman, because his course was charted and he didn't intend to trim his sails.

Next door, Rodney was getting out of the shower. He rubbed the towel thoroughly on his head with both hands, looked up at the mirror, stepped closer and took a long look at his tan and toned skin. "Not too bad, old man." He thought it was a good thing he remained loyal to his workouts and yoga routines. He didn't have any excess weight or flab. He was a manly man with broad shoulders and a narrow waist. He was six foot and one hundred-eighty pounds. He fingered his hair, glad that it was not receding like some of his colleagues. He decided to wear a black summer silk sports jacket, since they were dining in Peacock Alley. It was upscale and demanded a certain respect. Having a little time before he went next door to collect Dixie, he decided to make a couple of reservations. He sat in the study with a New York phone book and booked a tour that included Ground Zero, the Statue of Liberty, Rockefeller Center, and Times Square. He had to make the most of the time they had and show her a time she'd never forget. The following night he reserved balcony seats for a Broadway play, Backstreet Affair.

The concierge told the doctor and Dixie that it would be safe to take a brown bag lunch for a picnic while walking in Central Park. He told them of a safe spot to spread a blanket under a shady oak tree. He was very helpful, and Rodney was a generous tipper.

Dinner was divine. Rodney thanked the maitre d' for his superb suggestions, took Dixie's elbow, and led her to the exit. They decided to walk a few blocks and mill with the regular New Yorkers before they turned in. As the locals scurried by, Rodney told Dixie he loved the area and thought it would be a lovely place to live with so many interesting places and things to do. She agreed and pointed to a sign showing newly renovated condos. She asked if he'd like to check them out one afternoon before leaving. They were a high-rise, like most every building. After all, there was only so much space. Dixie picked up some information about when the condos would open and passed it to Rodney. They were both speechless. Then Rodney said, "Three thousand a month for a two bedroom!"

The hotel was situated on the corner of Park Avenue and Madison Avenue. Rodney told Dixie it was famous for its exclusive shops.

She wanted to get her bearings so she would know where she should go when he was at the hospital. They saw people scampering about, walking their dogs, taxis letting passengers out and picking up others. Rodney told Dixie that he wanted her to go shopping, and he was leaving her a credit card. She tried to resist but he insisted.

Finally, she agreed. She told him she'd like to visit the salon and spa at the hotel and get a full day beauty package. He thought that was a wonderful idea.

Returning to the Waldorf, the doorman greeted them. She thanked the doctor for everything. As he walked her to the big double door, she told him she would see him in the morning.

Dreamily, she thought of their week, she had not taken care of one detail. Dixie felt free as a bird. She dressed for bed but couldn't settle into slumber. She padded barefoot to the balcony. She was lost in the awe of her surroundings. Time was not a factor, but with heavy eyelids she was forced to return to the royal bed.

Chapter 20

Jettie called Joy on Wednesday. "Girlfriend, is it only three more weeks before the wedding?"

"Yes, can you believe it?"

"Is everything taken care of now?"

"I've hired a coordinator to organize and orchestrate everything regarding the wedding," Joy replied.

"What about food?"

"They've arranged a buffet with great food: smoked turkey and ham, vegetables, hot cobbler and hot yeast rolls and more. We're covered in that department. Everybody has rides to the house."

"Do they all have directions?" Jettie asked.

"We don't know how Dixie is supposed to get here, do we?" Joy asked.

"We'll have to ask her," Jettie said. "Do you think she should ride with someone or fly? I guess we just have to see if she has a plan."

Joy and Vince had made several trips to Tahoe in the last couple of weeks to check on all the furnishings, and had personally visited with many contractors regarding landscaping, security system, and all the man things that Vince took care of, for which Joy was glad.

Thursday morning, Rodney asked Dixie if she would like to have an early dinner in So Ho, then shop there for deep discount prices. They could walk over to Greenwich Village and roam through what used to be the number one draw during the Beatnik era with coffee houses, poetry and bra burning.

Eating breakfast on Friday morning, Rodney said to Dixie, "I love your new look. The hairstyle is so vogue." They both laughed.

Dixie had a stylist create her new do with deeper red hues.

She had her body wrapped, a European facial, manicure, pedicure, solar nails and her lashes tabbed. She then stood totally nude while the cosmetologist sprayed an instant tan on her. When she combined the look with her new wardrobe, you could tell she had been one busy woman.

Rodney was so generous. He insisted she buy three Versace pantsuits with shoes and bags to match, and jewelry for each ensemble. He enjoyed dressing her as much as she enjoyed dressing for him.

They were leaving for Dallas the following evening. He had a plan to ride the subway from Central Station to Connecticut, then returning and seeing Harlem, the Bronx and Brooklyn from the train.

Only one more night in that fabulous suite, but Dixie already had so many incredible memories. The trip had been better than she could have ever dreamed.

They discussed the offer at the hospital. Rodney said he was as impressed with the position, the facility, the salary, and the staff as he was the whole New York experience. "If I take it and move up in the next month, they would rent me the penthouse at the Waldorf for the first six months."

Late Friday night, they retired to their suites to pack, preparing to depart the next day. Dixie took all the clothes out of the drawers and bagged them. She felt she had been there for a long time. She felt a part of the city. She stopped, feeling the urge to go and look out over the city. It called and she obeyed.

She opened the French doors, left them wide and stood gazing at the streets and the little cars moving below. The gentle breeze kissed her cheek. City smells filled her nostrils. New York City was so alive she could feel its heartbeat. She now understood why people fell so in love with the Big Apple.

She heard a gentle tapping at the double doors. She peeped through the hole and saw Rodney. She wondered what was wrong. She opened the door with a look of concern.

"It's okay. I didn't mean to alarm you."

She motioned him to come in. He walked onto the terrace where she had been just minutes ago. They stood silently for several moments before he spoke. "Dixie, I can't leave here without telling you how I feel." He paused.

She stared at his face but said nothing.

He started to speak again, but held her shoulders with both hands and peered deeply into her eyes, "I don't know of any other way to say this, just simply, I love you. In fact, I'm desperately in love with you."

They looked at each other, and it felt as if the world stood still.

"Rodney," she said, "I feel the same way. I love you, but was afraid to admit it. You have been so wonderful to me as a doctor, and have such a generous heart."

He placed his fingertips to her lips. "Dixie, I've never wanted to put a woman on a pedestal before. Until you."

Tears came to her eyes, and his eyes grew moist as well. Their world stood still, they embraced each other and tenderly kissed, releasing a passion that could be restrained no longer. They fit perfectly, and it felt so good they never wanted to stop. But finally, they pulled back to look at each other.

"Dixie, I can't imagine life without you. I can't even think of how it was a few months ago before you came into my life. You're the only woman I've ever wanted to give the world. Will you do me the honor of being my wife?"

She could not quit looking at this beautiful man. There was no way she could resist him. "You name the time and day. I promise to be there." She squeezed him tightly and said, "It feels so right to be able to express my love for you."

They clung together between tears and laughter. Their hearts beat together, becoming one at that moment. On a terrace in upper Manhattan, a love affair was born.

"Dixie, I want you to marry me tomorrow."

Tears filled the eyes of the perky little redhead who was usually all fun, but at this moment, she was filled with emotion.

He went on, "We can fly to Niagara Falls, marry in the honeymoon capital of the world, and stay our honeymoon night at the Falls before flying home the next day. What do you say?"

"You make wonderful plans, so Niagara Falls, here we come." She smiled that big beautiful smile that he loved to see. She sang, "We're goin' to the chapel and we're gonna get married. We're goin' to the chapel of love." Hugging him, she swayed to her song.

Smiling, he said, "I want us to do this right, because it will be forever and until death we do part."

Hugging him and putting her head on his chest, she said in all seriousness, "You amaze me; I wouldn't have it any other way."

"I want us to go to Madison Avenue in the morning and pick out a ring."

"I can't wait! You're the most exciting man and too good to me."

He took her hand and headed to the big double doors. She was thrilled with his character. He did not intend to try and spend the night with her; he was the perfect man. She counted her blessings and thanked God for sending this wonderful man into her life. They kissed sweetly at the door.

"Darling, I will see you in the morning. Go to sleep and dream of me." Tenderly he pressed his lips to hers. "Good night." He held onto her outstretched hand as far as he could.

She smiled and swooned. Floating back to the royal bed, she knew he would be lying beside her tomorrow night and they would be together forever as man and wife. She gave into sweet slumber to dream of her handsome prince.

Settled in the plane bound for Niagara Falls, she had to pinch herself as she peeked in the box labeled Tiffany's that held the three-stone emerald-cut diamond ring. She would wear it in just a few hours to tell the world that they belonged to each other, Dr. and Mrs. Rodney Wallace! She had to close her eyes, then open them again to make sure this was not a beautiful dream. She was truly in heaven, and not just because she was flying United.

He leaned over, cupped her small hand protectively into his large one and gently squeezed. They approached 8,000 feet. The pilot announced, "You can see the majestic Falls on the right side of the plane, both the Canadian and the American Falls." It was unbelievable. She would have never guessed in a million years she would fly to Niagara Falls to marry.

As the minister quoted scripture, Dixie May was gripped by the seriousness of the ceremony. She glanced around, taking mental pictures, wanting to embrace this day forever. The quaint old church was appointed with stained glassed windows, rich wooden pews, and hymnals within reach.

"Rodney, do you take this woman to be your lawfully wedded wife?" She felt her heart might burst with emotion. "I do." Those were the two most beautiful words she had ever heard coming from such a loving and kind man as he.

He was instructed to put the ring on her finger. He never took his eyes from hers as he slid the chosen ring on her finger as he claimed her as his wife.

The minister continued, "Do you, Dixie, take this man to be your lawfully wedded husband?" She felt she might float from the floor. She was in heaven on earth with this, her soon-to-be husband forever. Tears trickled down her cheeks. Demurely, she answered, "I do."

She claimed him with the simple band of gold that slipped onto his well-groomed finger. The minister finished by saying, "I now pronounce you man and wife. You may kiss your bride."

Immediately, they wrapped themselves around the other and swayed for a moment. Tenderly and knowingly, their lips met for the first time as man and wife. They agreed to love and cherish forever and sealed it with a kiss.

Dixie would always be able to count on Rodney to do the right thing. His manners were impeccable; he extended his hand to the minister and said, "Sir, we want to thank you and your lovely wife for everything—a splendid job, and especially for joining me with my beautiful bride."

Briskly walking down the aisle, Dixie stopped, turned, and tossed the bouquet to the precious little woman standing by the piano.

Niagara Falls would forever be a special memory in their hearts. Every year they planned to return and keep the memories alive. The romantic bungalow that Rodney chose for their honeymoon night was unique; Michaels Inn of the Falls was the perfect setting to begin their lives on that wondrous night at the magnificent Falls. One of the seven natural wonders of the world spread across the horizon, and they had the pleasure of being a part of it.

The very first morning of their married life, the newlyweds had breakfast in bed. Neither wanted to leave the other for even a moment. Soon they would be on the flight back to Dallas. "It will take hell and high water to keep me from having a honeymoon tour with my new wife through the wine country before we go back to the USA." She listened to her man make their plans, and she was at peace with the world. They finished their breakfast and decided they must start every morning with breakfast in bed. The tour started in an hour, so they wrapped it up and headed to the shower together.

Chapter 21

The plane touched down at DFW at ten a.m. Dallas time. The valet delivered the Mercedes, and they headed east on Interstate 30 to Chapel Valley, by way of Silver Springs. Dixie had to check on the beauty shop, then stop by her house and pick up a few items. She planned to stay in Dallas at Rodney's home in the White Rock Lake area. They had less than three weeks to get settled in Manhattan. So many exciting events were taking place she didn't know how it would feel, but she had no desire to make it stop.

"I must call Jettie."

He reached in his jacket, handed her his cell phone, and said with a wink, "Anything for my bride."

Smiling back at him, she took the phone and dialed Jettie's office, knowing she was going to catch it for being out of touch. The girls were going to be worried, and she understood.

Jettie was concerned, seeing the doctor's name on her phone. "Dr. Wallace, is everything all right? We can't find Dixie."

"It's me, Jettie. I'm okay."

"What? Where have you been? We've been out of our minds, girl. And why is this call coming in as Dr. Wallace's number?"

"Jettie, settle down and listen. I'm fine, and on my way home. I want you to get Joy and meet me at the Enchanted Gardens at one o'clock sharp. We must have an emergency heart-to-heart. I can't answer any more questions right now. I'm using his phone, but I will see ya'll there, okay?"

Jettie, confused, reluctantly answered, "Well, okay. I'll find Joy and pick her up. We'll be there one way or another."

"I love you, Jettie."

"I love you too, girl."

Joy had a million questions for Jettie.

"Joy, I don't know anything else. I have no idea where she's been," Jettie said for at least the third time during the ride to the tea room. They parked in the lot. The crowd looked minimal, but there was no sign of Dixie. They got out and went in, making a potty stop, then settled into their regular table.

They had drunk about half a glass of their tea when a strange black Mercedes pulled into the drive and parked next to their car. They craned their necks. Never saying a word to each other, they watched. When the driver's door opened, they were surprised to see Dr. Wallace, but he was dressed quite differently than usual. Instead of a white hospital jacket, he wore a lightweight sports jacket and slacks. They followed his walk to the passenger side and he opened the door. The most stunning woman, wearing a sage designer pantsuit that was to die for, stepped from the car. She had a bronze tan that looked like she had been on the beaches of Hawaii, and a chic hairstyle you saw on runway models. She reeked of New York City.

Joy and Jettie sat there, speechless with their mouths hanging open. Dr. Wallace escorted Dixie May to the table. The girls were bowled over with her newly acquired style and beauty.

"My God, you are breathtaking," Jettie said. The women were up in a flash with their arms around one another in the heart-to-heart huddle.

Once over the shock, they settled down and wiped tears from one another's faces. Dixie said, "Jettie, Joy, you remember Dr. Wallace?"

Joy said, "Well, of course." Her eyebrows were drawn, as in a question.

Dixie continued, "Oh that's right, but I don't believe that you've met my husband, Rodney."

They all screamed; it was a circus. With tears of joy and shock, they wept and laughed. When they managed to calm down, they wanted all the details, the trip, how it all happened and how did they plan to elope to Niagara Falls?

Joy said, "You couldn't have done anything that would have shocked me more."

"I can't wait to tell Camilla and Krystal; they are going to die!" Jettie said.

"I have a lot to tell ya'll," Dixie said. "We're moving to Manhattan in the penthouse at the Waldorf that Rodney stayed in while in Manhattan, for the first six months. We have plans to locate us a condo in the same area, the heart of the city, and we only have three weeks to get moved! Rodney has put his house on the market, in the hands of a well-established realtor."

Jettie tried to say something, but Dixie put her finger up to stop her and kept talking. "My house in Chapel Valley is already with a real estate company. The salon has been sold to Wanda; it worked out well for all. And, Illiana Winn gave Wanda a good deal on a three-year lease. Whew, okay, now you can talk."

Jettie wanted to know if they were planning on attending the Tahoe wedding, and Dixie squealed, "Of course! You know I wouldn't miss it for anything." She grabbed Rodney's hand. "Neither would my sweet husband."

He smiled and nodded in agreement.

Later that evening, Jettie and Joy were on the phone calling friends. They could hardly talk about Tahoe for discussing Dixie and Rodney. There was a lot to talk about, because Dixie and the doctor's elopement had stolen the thunder, and a lot of information was not discussed regarding the Tahoe wedding.

Joy said to Jettie, "Wanda told Dixie during the salon sale that Peter Winn was sentenced to two life sentences with no chance of parole. He has already been sent to Huntsville. His wife planned to sell out and return to her hometown just south of St. Louis. " After rehashing the Peter Winn news, the ladies managed to get the final details together and discussed the arrival plans of the friends and relatives for the first time.

Joy and Vince would fly to Tahoe a few days early and be there if any last minute details popped up. The Tahoe wedding was only eleven days away. Joy told Jettie to make sure that all knew to fly into Reno and reserve a rental, then drive the thirty miles to Tahoe.

"Toby and I will be flying down very early the morning of the wedding day," Jettie said. "Ben will pilot us to the wedding and back home on his Cessna directly into Reno. Krystal and Johnny plan to leave DFW and will stay an extra three days to take in the sights."

The girls laughed because they knew that Krystal would always make the most of the circumstances, and they would be doing Tahoe before their return to Texas. They hooted, "You know Krystal will have the candles and matches packed."

Camilla and Rocky would board an American Airlines plane from Intercontinental with a direct flight to Reno, and drive down to the Lake. All the other people, like Jules and Chauncey, other relatives that could make it, and a few of their business acquaintances were all to meet at Joy and Vince's new home in Truckee. That would allow them time to visit for several hours before dressing for the late afternoon wedding. Joy's wedding gown was bought in Dallas, where Jettie and Joy did the circuit, searching for the perfect gown.

The McNamaras arrived with Ben. "He was quite the pilot," Jettie said to Toby. Arriving early, they parked in a small private hanger in Truckee. Vince and Joy were waiting to greet their Texas buddies. Jettie was the matron of honor and Toby the best man. The girls needed a little extra time to get it all together; besides, this was going to be hard when everything settled down. Jettie realized Dixie May was way up in New York and Joy was way up in northern California. So much had happened in the last four months, it was hard to keep up. It gave Toby reason to be concerned about Jettie.

Vince would be a perfect groom in his white tux with tails, tanned good looks, and sun-kissed blond hair. The impressive Blue Wave three-deck Cabin Cruiser would be the setting. The impressive forty-five-foot yacht would cruise out into the lake, hosting forty family members and friends. The cabin cruiser would be docked at Zephyr Cove, tied to the long pier, as the crew made repeated trips with flowers, wine and food.

The musicians would arrive thirty minutes prior to the scheduled time. The minister would release three white doves representing the newlyweds being escorted toward a heavenly union. Pictures would be taken. Joy and Vince would remain in their wedding clothes, prepared to be showered with rice and shouts of gaiety as they made their way to their White Escalade and headed to their new home that awaited the new Mr. and Mrs. Vincent Chandler. Vince would carry his beautiful bride over the threshold at last. It was all coming together so perfectly.

Vince drove Toby and Ben around, showing them the things men like to see. He pointed out where movies had been made, fishing areas, and where the trails headed up the mountain. And, of course, Toby had to see the road that led to the casinos.

Jettie and Joy headed back to the house, and the cell phones were ringing. Everyone checked in as they arrived, needing more directions from Reno to Truckee. Camilla and Rocky headed to their hotel to unpack. They planned to dress for the wedding and would come to the house, visit a while, then follow the caravan to the Cove. Camilla said they saw Krystal and Johnny on the road driving up from Reno. She got Krystal on the phone and had them follow them to the house, because Jettie felt they might have a hard time finding it alone.

The girls had five hours before the guests would start arriving. They were both exhausted. Joy said, "Let's hurry up so we can grab a quick nap. I'm taking my bubble bath to unwind these tight muscles." Jettie wholeheartedly agreed and said she would do the same.

Joy hired a service of five to cater to the guests and tend to their needs. There was sliced roasted turkey and honey baked ham, a large variety of vegetables, including red beans and corn bread, a delicious selection of sweets, banana pudding, peach cobbler, hot yeast rolls, and a soft serve machine for ice cream. She counted on folks being hungry after making the trip. There would be champagne and cake at the reception with finger foods at the resort, then dancing and picture taking.

Joy was anxious to see Jules; she hadn't seen her in a couple of weeks, and this would be the first time for Jules to see her mom's new home. It would be a happy, yet sad time, as miles would separate the pair.

Chapter 22

Vince looked at his watch and announced it was two p.m. "Time to head to Zephyr Cove. It will take us about twenty minutes to get there. And, they instructed us to be onboard by three forty-five."

Once aboard they would cruise for two hours. The crowd hustled to their vehicles and formed a line. They caravan started down the road that partially circled the lake. It was exciting; the fresh mountain air invigorating. It was a magnificent day for a wedding long overdue. Joy looked radiant. Her shiny hair hugged her shoulders just the way Vince liked it. Her gown was an original design by Elani. The exquisite beading and lace bodice gave subtle hints of prism pink. It flowed to the floor in a fishtail train, with covered buttons to the low back and built-in corset. Jewels sparkled between the spaghetti straps and the veil floated gently around her face.

Joy had never seen a wedding like this, nor had the guests. It was a first for all. And that added to the excitement—charting courses they had never known. Once everyone had boarded, the crew released the rope, and they were set free, headed to the middle of the picturesque lake. After reaching their destination, the boat was set to idle and the ceremony began. The lapping sounds of water were tranquil as the pictures were taken throughout the service.

The minister wore a captain's uniform as befit for the occasion. The actual formality of the service moved along swiftly, then they exchanged matching diamond bands of white gold. Joy handed her pastel bouquet to Jettie while she placed the ring on Vince's finger, her tiny hands shaking. It was sweet and romantic. The minister instructed the groom to kiss the bride. Vince took her face in his hands and tenderly touched his lips to hers. Then they held each other for the first time as man and wife. Hands joined and facing each other as if no one were around, they exchanged verses of a poem they had written. Vince, feeling the need to touch her face, gently brushed her cheek with the back of his hand.

There wasn't a dry eye on the boat. The long separated lovers committed the rest of their lives to each other on that beautiful yacht, in the middle of the famous lake, a thousand miles away from where the bashful teens first met. Still holding hands, they stood looking deeply into each other's eyes. The angelic voice of the late Karen Carpenter filled the air; the lapping water swayed the boat, caressing the wedding party to, "We've Only Just Begun."

At the appropriate time the minister announced, "It is with great pleasure that I introduce Mr. and Mrs. Vincent Chandler."

Jules was the first to grab her mama as a stream of tears rolled down her face.

"Honey, please don't cry." Joy softly dried her tears.

"Mama, these are happy tears. I feel so good about your life now, and I know in my heart that Vince will take care of you."

The two women embraced. Vince put his arms around the two most important women in his life. "Sweetheart, I will always love and take care of your mama; never worry." Vince kissed Jules. It felt good to be a family.

At that point, cute little Joy, feeling happy and gay, gave a perfect smile and curtsied to her audience. The handsome groom followed suit and took a bow. The Texas party animals let their feelings be known as the whistles and cheers echoed in the Cove.

More pictures were taken and the garter was thrown, as well as the bouquet—a friend of Jules was the thrilled recipient. When the boat docked at Zephyr Cove, they prepared to exit. It was short jaunt up the mountain to the resort. Most of the guests were from Texas, and they were wowed by the scenic beauty that surrounded them.

The gang waited for the last car before they made their way to the elevators, which only held eight at a time. Jettie and Camilla were some of the first to arrive on the tenth floor. They walked into the open reception area, which featured a glorious view of the sparkling blue lake from the towering terrace. It was time to have fun and celebrate. Tables and chairs were abundant and a jukebox stood in the corner, a special request of the bride. The music blared, and the dancers hit the floor, making the most of their time to let the good times roll. .

"Good job," Jettie said, and pulled Joy to the side. "Joy, we love you, me and Toby both, and we are so very happy for you and Vince. We know this is exactly what you've always wanted. But, we can only stay about thirty minutes, then we have to head home before it gets too late. Ben doesn't feel comfortable pushing it by waiting too late to fly that far. Well, the real truth is, I don't feel comfortable flying in that tiny plane late at night."

Joy told her she understood and made her promise to come back real soon. "I love you like my sister."

Jettie nodded. They hugged and held each other, knowing it was going to be different now. They would be states away, but they would be okay; they had the guys and planned to visit each other often.

The jukebox was cranked up. A wedding cake was decorated with a bride and groom sitting in a boat. It was precious and unique.

Jettie and Camilla sneaked a big fancy bottle into the kitchen, and nobody paid any attention to them. Jettie told Camilla that she and Toby, along with Ben, would be leaving shortly as they had to be back in Texas for business.

Camilla's smile evaporated. "You are going to miss so much fun!"

Jettie in defense blurted, "Entrepreneur woman, now, listen to yourself, we have to make a living!"

Camilla hugged Jettie. "I know, honey. I will just miss you and hate to see you miss all the fun. I totally understand. Believe me, I do."

The last picture taken with Vinnie and Joy standing by the cake.

"Everyone get a glass and prepare for a toast," Dixie said.

Camilla and Rocky stood by Joy and Vince. Dixie handed Rocky the bottle. Camilla helped him slip off the black velvet bag. "Joy and Vince, we met you a lifetime ago, forty years to be exact, and today we celebrate a new beginning. We have a special gift for

Heart to Heart ♥ Forever

you, our special friends, on this most joyous occasion. Camilla, will you do the honors?"

Without hesitation, she took the bottle displaying the eloquently designed label. "We present a bottle of our finest, expressly named for you, the exquisite Rossi di Jo Vinitti."

Oohs and aahs resonated throughout the room. The dignified and stunning Camilla, in her rich Italian accent, said, "Can I get a Yee Haw?"

And of course the Texans let them rip.

The newlyweds were honored with the Fenittis' generosity and humbly accepted.

Wine was passed around. When it was done, Rocky made a toast to the newlyweds. The guests were impressed with the generosity of the Fenittis' thoughtful gift.

Jettie announced their departure. She told the group to refill their glasses and wait for them on the terrace. "I want to see you all as long as I can. We'll be flying by in the red Cessna. You won't miss us. Prepare to make a toast when you see us."

With mixed emotions, the girlfriends formed a circle, the last one for a long time. They didn't know when there would be another heart-to-heart. Tears trickled.

Toby grabbed Jettie's hand and off they went. Looking back over her shoulder, with Toby pulling her along, Jettie shouted, "I love ya'll."

About fifteen minutes after they left, the gang moved to the terrace to wait. In just a few minutes, they grew quiet, "Listen," Vince said, "I hear them coming."

All eyes stared in the direction of the strange sound. The little red plane circled the building close enough to see Jettie and Toby with champagne glasses raised for the toast. The well-wishers waved, and some of the girls blew kisses to the McNamaras.

There was a movement at the tail of the Cessna. Fear gripped the rowdy bunch. Silence fell over the merry makers as they watched spellbound.

"What's happening?" Dixie asked with a strained voice.

Then, in full view, a long banner unfolded and trailed directly behind the plane with bold lettering that read, "Heart-to-heart ~ Forever."

Dixie May's shrill voice could be heard above all the noise on the balcony. "Oh, how cute!" She clapped her hands and pointed. "Look at that!"

The sighs of relief and jubilation in the same moment was just like their lives—a roller coaster. The girls were thrilled and let it be known by their reaction. They raised their glasses toward the McNamaras and shouted in unison, "Heart-to-heart ~ Forever," then tossed back the wine, as the little red plane disappeared into the white puffy clouds.

The End

Join us now for a sneak preview of Kay's next book . . .

Illiana

The first time Illiana Westbrook laid eyes on Samuel DeMarco, she dubbed him Sampson for his strength in the courtroom. Not only was he good to look at, he'd made her a seven-figure settlement. A rich oil widow at the Country Club had recommended him, and Illiana immediately called and made an appointment. He would represent her estate and file her divorce. They were on the phone a dozen times the first day.

After receiving her final decree, they stood on the courthouse steps. His white hair blew slightly; he smoothed it with his large tan hand. "Illiana, I'm glad you heeded my advice and changed your name." He reached over and laid his hand on her shoulder. "Leave this hell behind and be glad you can." He took his hand and cupped her chin to lift her eyes to meet his own. "Beautiful lady, you can have the world on a string." A big smile exposed perfect teeth. His eyes crinkled at the corner and his baby blue eyes seemed to twinkle.

He is one handsome man, she thought. Women hung onto his every word in the courtroom, and every head turned when he entered a room; his distinguished presence just demanded it.

Illiana took his hand and covered it with her own. "Dear Sampson, during the trial, how could I have endured without you by my side?"

He nodded. "I will only be a phone call away if you ever need me."

They walked down the last step of the old courthouse. He kissed her hand, and they parted, heading in separate directions. Another goodbye.

Illy vowed she would never tell her parents about the double murders her husband committed. She would simply say, "We fell out of love and grew apart."

She had promised the realtor she would leave the keys in the kitchen. This would be her final task—and the final nail in the coffin of her fifteen-year marriage.

Despite the tears clouding her eyes and the sadness that hovered over her, she was anxious to leave. She glanced about, then secured the door and left. Outside, the breeze fluttered and birds sang—something she once enjoyed but today left her empty.

Illiana Westbrook watched the city limit sign reduce to a speck in her rear view mirror. She floored her Pearl White BMW and headed eastbound out of Chapel Valley; she'd make St. Louis by nightfall. With her brows taut and her lips pursed, she assessed her life. It paralleled the speck. On a scale from one to ten, her life had been a ten plus. In a matter of days, it had been squashed to zero.

She missed Peter and their passionate intimacy. They might have had other problems, but lovemaking was not one of them. She was anxious to again feel desirable. She had no intention of becoming an embittered old woman.

Illiana had big plans on the drawing board. She'd purchased an old mansion about five miles from her folks that soon would be ready to move in. And her new business, Westbrook Interiors, was about ready to open. Adrenalin rushed for the first time in years.

Still a looker at thirty-five, Illiana was often compared to Audrey Hepburn, hailed as the most beautiful woman in history. Illiana possessed the same qualities. Lithe and agile, she had the grace of a swan and the body of a ballerina. Her walk exuded sensuality; long legs that pranced precisely, effortlessly, causing men to drool. No Hollywood star could beat her; she was stunning.